<u>*KHARMA*</u>

<u>*Deadly Demise*</u>

<u>*A Sequel to Kharma's Child*</u>

<u>*Inked By*</u>

<u>*Vette & KS Oliver*</u>

Bridget
Thank you
for your
support
KSO

1

Copyright ©2016 Vette Wilson & KS Oliver

Edited by Brandi Jefferson

Cover Designed by Aija Monique of AMB Branding

Published by Diamante' Publications, LLC

www.diamantepublications.com

DEDICATION FROM VETTE

I dedicate this book and every other that I ink to my children Diamyon (S.I.P), Joshua, Aliyah, Miracle, Diashya, Lola, and Lorenzo Jr. Everything I do is for all of you. Thank you for the motivation and drive.
I love each of you.

DEDICATION FROM *K.S. OLIVER*

I dedicate this book and every other that I ink to my husband B. you are more than just the love of my life but my friend and my biggest supporter.

To my children (KS) Kwan & Shaun. We did it again. I can't thank the two of you enough for teaching me every day about what it is to truly love unconditionally. Thank you for picking me of all people to be your mom. I am truly blessed.
My brother Siyn, you are the last one I have left and I am my brother's keeper.

To my brothers Ajmal Acklin, and Jarvis Jones (S.I.P).
Last but not least to my brother Khayree Y. Acklin I had the pleasure of being involved in 19 years of your life before you were taken away. I can't believe that I won't get that call from you today saying hey sis your book dropped yet? That's ok I know I am making you proud of me. My birthday will never be the same but I promise to keep reaching towards the top just like you would have wanted me to.

I now I have the best angels in the business. I feel untouchable.

ACKNOWLEDGEMENTS FROM VETTE

First and foremost I would like to thank My God. This has been a long journey but it is only just beginning. I also dedicate this Book to every woman that has ever fallen in love with the wrong man.

Special thanks to my Diamante' Publications Family. You guys keep me grounded and on the right path. It feels good to know that I have so much support and the biggest part of that support starts with you all. To my Diamante' brother Willie Leblanc you are one of the strongest yet stubborn guys I know. You have strength that I as a woman admire thanks for listening when I needed that big brother talk. Sis Marissa Palmer you are so pure at heart. The spiritual guidance I have received from you is nothing short of amazing and for that I am forever grateful. Shatika Turner you are a very tough woman. You never allow anything or anyone hinder you. You work harder than any editor/promoter I know. Thank you for taking this journey with me. King Diamond well it has been my pleasure in getting to know you. You have no filter but that in my book is a good thing. Shout out Tavon Wilson I hear your pen is on fire little bro. Your time is short keep pushing.

To the bosses of Diamante' oh wow! Ebonee' Oliver you are one of the hardest working women in this publishing game. When you crack that whip believe me it is heard miles around. Thank you for pushing me. You give me Tough love and you are very dear to my heart. Brandon I have to thank you and thank you again because had it not been for you I wouldn't have been able to work with such an amazing woman.

To my cousin Alyssa Wilson. Thank you for believing in me and supporting me in everything I do.

Shout out to my readers and my supporters without you guys this wouldn't be possible I love each and every one of you.

A huge thanks to Aija for making all of my Covers. They are everything I imagine and more thank you love.

To all of the promoters and test readers that had a hand in reading promoting my books thank you all so much I humbly appreciate it all.

ACKNOWLEDGEMENTS FROM KS OLIVER

I want to first thank God for keeping me and Blessing me with the ability to write a story. I've been through it all and some, but it has only humbled me and made me even stronger. I am made of bricks now.

To my parents (Clarine & C.O) and my grandparents (Mary & Woody Oliver), my mother in law Rose Abby, my sister in law Claudette Davis, my step dad Leroy White and my step mom Desiree Thornton- Oliver. Last but not least my mother from another Sharyn Whitfield. Thank you for everything. You have supported me in everything I have set out to do. I appreciate each of you and the unique things that you bring out of me.

A Huge thank you to Aija Butler for a great cover once again. I appreciate you as a designer and a friend. You always help me bring my story to life.

Thank you to my day 1's, LeTorri Mitchell, Reynica Young, Kim Stone, Latrice Burns, Nadia Brown, Karen Cabret, LaChaun Tucker, Dominique Watson, Karessa Martin and Aunt Minnie (Leigh McKnight).

To my brothers from another Jacorey Oneal, Jeremiah Jones and Rashad Bligen. I love y'all down. Time flies and the sky is the limit. Hold your head up and keep going its almost over.

S/O to the Literary Ladies of the ATL Kenni York, Kierra Petty, and Nika Michelle. Thank you for always being there when I needed you and when I didn't. My sisters in Lit and boy do we act the part. We don't always get along but I love you all.

Thank you to all of my readers. Special S/O to Brandi Jefferson, Lanae Evans, Melanie Moses, Priscilla Murray, Angelina Butler and Natasha Hill. I couldn't do this without y'all.

Diamonds are forever and so is my team. Shout out to Diamante' Publications. King Diamond, Janae M. Robinson, Shatika Turner, B. Abby, Tavon Wilson, Willie LeBlanc and Vonda Roche' thanks to all of you for the constant support. Last but not least my mini me and codefendant Vette, we do this.

PROLOGUE

"Honey I'm home," were the words that sweetly sang out of Kharma Gomez's mouth as he struggled to regain focus. The knock on the head had caused him to be very dazed and off balance. He knew that Kharma had come back to avenge her torn and broken heart but will she have enough heart left to allow him to see his children ever again?

CHAPTER 1
(*DEADLY DEMISE*)

Adam struggled to open his eyes as he began to regain consciousness. The warm rays from the sun burned his eyes as he carefully opened them. The floor felt unusually soft and firm as he felt for something to pull himself up on to his feet. Just then he noticed that his head rested upon a pillow and not the cold hardened floor. Adam continued to feel until he noticed that his wife was beside him in her usual place aside him in bed or so he thought.

"Lana, sweetheart wake up. Baby I had the most fucked up dream and it's really messing with me right now." Adam was soft spoken he had no clue that his nightmare was much more than just a dream.

"Baby?" As he gently pulled the woman whom he thought to be his wife closer to him, he heard an all too familiar voice call out to him.

"Awwwww what's the matter sweetie, did the Boogeyman frighten you?" The strange woman let out a sinister laugh as Adam, startled, jumped back so fast he fell off the bed and on to the floor.

"KHARMA!" He yelled as she got out the bed and stood over him as he sat frozen with fear on the floor.

"Miss me baby?" Kharma smiled as she positioned herself beside Adam and began to crawl all over him as to seduce him.

"You crazy bitch how did you get in my house?" he asked her. Kharma was not in the mood for small talk. As far as she was concerned, he was the one who was crazy making her love him and then leaving her and their baby just like that.

"Get off me damn it!" He shoved Kharma into the side of the bed.

"Adam stop it!"

"How could you ask that question when you know exactly how I got in here? I mean I should hope that I would find a way into my own home. Don't you think so?" Kharma was somehow convinced that she was in fact home and she owed no one an explanation.

"You are one psycho bitch if you honestly think that any of what me and my wife share could ever belong to you. Look at you stressing over what and who you could never be. Kharma, you'll never be Lana or Mrs. Adam D Harris," Adam assured an uneasy Kharma who was by now red in the face. What were these things that the man she had given her innocence to saying? Kharma was in a world of false hope if she honestly thought that Adam would ever love her.

"Adam I know what this is, you're spicing up our sex life with role play. Okay sweetie I'll play along, now what is my character's name. Wait. I know how about I play Kacey and you can

play---"

"Shut up!" Adam interrupted Kharma who was purposely taunting him about Kacey.

Kharma, you need help. We, you and I, are not a couple. You are not my wife. This is not your home and I will never love you. All you were was an easy escape from my wife when she was being a worldly bitch, but now that things between she and I are better I could not imagine spending the rest of my life without her."

Kharma stood in a trance as she suddenly let out a smirk and before Adam could blink Kharma was around his throat with a sharp kitchen knife pressing it deeply into his Adam's apple.

"You know Mayor Harris you are just like so many men. See, you want your cake and ice cream all in the same damn plate. I am sorry baby, but it just doesn't work that way. See if I can't have you then you are of no use to me alive." Kharma began to dig the knife deeper into his throat but fate that day for her was not on her side.

"I don't think so bitch," a stern feminine voice called out to Kharma Gomez.

"Lana, nice of you to join us. We were just discussing you." Kharma smiled as she continued to hold the knife underneath Adam's throat.

Had she been paying any attention she would have seen the lime green colored .38 glock handgun that Lana was gripping tightly in her left hand.

"I swear I have little respect for you young girls these days always falling in love with outside dick that will never belong to you. Look at you, so pitiful."

Adam who was very relieved to see his wife didn't miss the loaded weapon he had purchased for her just months ago.

"LANA, now would be a good damn time to take this bitch out!" Adam demanded his wife.

Lana smiled at her husband and took one look at Kharma and suddenly fired two shots past Kharma and into her and Adam's wedding portrait that was placed on the wall next to the balcony door.

"Jesus Lana! What the hell is wrong with you, I said her not me. Damn it you almost took my head off," a shaken up Adam cried out to Lana who was still holding the smoking gun.

"Oh my darling husband I'm sorry, did I frighten you?" Lana asked sarcastically.

"You know Adam, I never could understand why you chose to go scavenger hunting when you have your steak and potatoes right here," Lana subliminally hinted toward Kharma.

"Wait who in the hell are you calling a scavenger bitch. Don't think that just because your ass is holding that gun you are not prone to getting that ass kicked." Kharma, now face to face with Lana Harris, wasn't about to let this bitch come in here and ruin her plans or intimidate her.

"Oh how cute, it speaks and it fucks my husband. Tell me Adam, what other tricks does your pet do?" Lana laughed at Kharma's petty threat.

"So what is this Lana? Huh? You're here to kill me, or did you just want to sit and stare in the pretty ass face of the woman who had your hubby eating the booty like groceries?" Kharma smirked as she shook her ass in Adam's face. Adam pushed her off as to show his wife that he didn't want anything to do with Kharma or her booty, well not anymore at least.

"Not a chance young Kharma, see the

dick was good, but the money and power feels even better understand. It's time you stop thinking with that kitty of yours and with your head." Lana was trying to educate Kharma on the game of life.

"Lana you're in on this sadistic shit. You are my wife, we have children together, what are they going to think?" Adam asked as if he had a right to ask any questions or have any kinds of hurt feelings.

"You mean what would Aimee think if she found out that the low life she calls daddy is not her father at all?" Lana had no remorse after spilling the tea to Adam the way she did.

Kharma who just as shocked as Adam was, took a step back and began to study Lana up and down before saying "Damn bitch hats off to you and here I thought you were some housewife, but you are my shero." Kharma laughed at the big ass pill Adam was about to swallow.

Adam finally found his strength and with all the power he could muster he got on his feet shoved past Kharma and without warning slapped Lana so hard the impact knocked her into the wooden door that led into the hallway

"You fucking whore!" He yelled out in hurt and anger.

Lana smiled as she flipped her hair from her face and with one finger wiped the blood that covered her bottom lip. Kharma felt remorse for a weeping Adam and for the life of her she tried to justify as to why these old feelings were emerging once more.

Kharma pulled Lana to the side to gain some insight to what she had just heard.

"Lana, correct me if I'm wrong but weren't you the same one who had so much to say about me becoming pregnant and leaving work Ms. High and fake ass mighty!" Kharma said out of mockery.

"Oh save me the small talk!" And before Kharma could say another word Lana quickly turned to Adam and empty her clip into his chest.

POW

POW

POW

POW

The gun that Lana Harris used to murder her unfaithful husband didn't make much noise as Lana had the smarts to place a silencer on it to seal out any sounds. Adam fell to floor after the third shot that was fired at him. Lana decided to bask in all her glory by taking a selfie with her deceased hubby.

"Kharma was at a standstill and was in a trance at this entire ordeal. Sure she wanted Adam to pay for what he had done but some part of her still loved him.

"Kharma, Kharma helllooo earth to Kharma, wake up heffa!" Lana snapped her fingers in front of Kharma's face to gain her attention.

"Catch!" Lana tossed the gun into Kharma's hands, who then snapped back into reality and allowed the smoking gun to fall to the floor.

"ARE YOU FUCKING CRAZY, WHY DID YOU DO THAT?" Kharma cried out in a state of panic.

"Do what, put a stray dog to sleep? Isn't that what they do at the pet shop somewhere?" Lana asked showing little remorse.

"YES, BUT THAT'S FOR ANIMALS LANA!" Kharma exclaimed

"Animals, Adam, what's the difference again? Lana nonchalantly questioned.

"And to call the kettle black Kharma, You had no right to kill my husband." Sounding like a weeping widow, Lana Harris gathered her purse and car keys and calmly walked out the master bedroom.

Kharma collected her thoughts, tossed a sheet over Adam's body and hurried after Lana who was just about to drive off.

"Lana, wait." She called out.

"What did you mean back there? Are you insinuating that I killed Adam when clearly we know who pulled that trigger?!"

"Of course we do Kharma. You broke into our home, stole my gun from my closet, and fired bullets into my husband's chest." Lana had obviously thought this through very well.

"No you killed your husband. This is crazy Lana, no one will ever believe you!" Kharma became agitated at the thought of Lana framing her for Adam's death, but she knew she'd be the only one to have a damn good motive to actually do this to his trifling ass.

"Oh by the way, on the subject of no one believing me in this situation you may want to rethink that boo let us not forget whose prints are on that weapon." Lana was now out of her car and standing face to face and nose to nose with her now deceased hubby's side chick, made clear to the now and once again victimized Kharma.

"NO, YOUR PRINTS ARE THE ONLY ONES ON THAT DAMN GUN,
I NEVER TOUCHED IT!"

"Oh but I think you did Ms. Gomez." Lana laughed sarcastically got back and into her car and drove off; throwing a single black rose out onto the pavement and yelling "HERE,

LOOKS LIKE YOU MAY NEED THIS BACK!" at Kharma while driving off.

Kharma couldn't fight back the tears that had been welding up in her eyes since she saw the love of her life fall onto that bed and take his last breath. Kharma couldn't shake the image of Adam reaching out his hand to her as Lana filled his chest with bullet after bullet. She slowly picked the rose from the stone pavement and proceeded to walk slowly back into the now silenced mansion. The hall seemed to grow longer and longer as she got closer to where Adam Harris rested his head. The sight nearly made Kharma sick to the stomach. Sure the man lying in that pool of blood that stained the sheets on the bed once broke her heart, he once killed her soul and spirit as a woman, but now that he was gone the baby boy that she share with this man will never get to know or see his father. Kharma slowly walked up to the shell that was once Adam and placed the single rose upon Adam's chest near his heart and quietly left the Mayor's mansion leaving behind faded memories of her and Adam.

CHAPTER 2
(A Mother's Love)

Kharma walked for almost an hour trying to figure out her next move; in doing this she barely noticed her phone ringing. "Whoever this is it is not the time for conversations." Kharma said to herself not knowing that the person on the other end of that phone call would be who she least expected.

"Hello, who is this," she tried to sound at ease.

"Kharma Gomez you mean to tell me that you do not recognize the voice of your own mother anymore," Melita softly asked her daughter.

"Mom, I have never been so happy to hear your voice. Things have gotten so out of control and well look I rather not say over the phone can you meet me somewhere?" Kharma asked her mother.

"Kharma you know better than that. You know where home is, it hasn't been that long, I'll see you in a little while." Melita assured Kharma.

Kharma finally found a bus stop and decided to wait on the next bus heading in her old neighborhood. She was nervous about going back there and facing her family after the way she just up and left without a proper goodbye. The bus showed after twenty minutes of running late and after just 35 mins she was finally back home. The sidewalks looked as if they had been painted or redone in that short period of time of her being gone and the houses seemed smaller and closer together.

Finally she had made it home. As she stood there in front of the driveway she realized that home didn't seem like home anymore either.

"Well, are you going to go in or are just going to run away again?" a man's voice whispered in her ear; she turned slowly to find that it was Alonzo and as always he was being the pest of a brother he had always been.

"Lonzoooo, oh my god you are such a pest baby bro!" Kharma said while hugging her brother.

"Okay that's enough of that touchy feeling stuff." Alonzo pushed his big sister away and shoved her playfully causing Kharma to chase him upon the porch and into the front door where her mother and father awaited her arrival.

The house looked the same. The furniture seemed brand new.

"Kharma, welcome back home sweetheart your dad and I have been waiting on you and I cooked your favorite pasta," Melita said while tightly hugging her daughter.

"Princess I hope you're hungry your mother's been in that kitchen cooking up a storm." Sebastian bragged while greeting his daughter with a hug as well. Kharma was reluctant to sit down to dinner with her family. She knew that they would have questions and at that moment the last thing she needed was to be interrogated about Adam and her relationship with him and their love child.

"Smells good mom. So what's up, how's Alonzo doing in school?" Kharma asked her father while her brother washed up from playing football with his friends all day.

"Oh well he's improving, he just needs to study more and keep his head in the books, and out of I mean off of the girls." Sebastian clears his throat as Melita gives him the side eye. Kharma becomes silent all of a sudden and gazes off into her own world. She continued to replay the image of Adam reaching out his hand to her over and over again.

"Sweetheart are you okay?" Melita asked out of concern.

"What do you mean mom I'm fine," Kharma responded.

"Listen Kharma you don't have to hide anything from us. We love you, we are your family, and we will not judge you."
Melita said to her now irritated daughter.
"See this is why I didn't want to come back here. God, can't you just let it be mother. Yes I fucked Adam, a married official. Yes I got myself knocked up and yes he left me alone and confused. I lived, I cried, and damn it I have learned!"
Kharma angrily scolded her mother.
"Wait a minute, first off Kharma I'm going to need you to bring that tone down. Let's be clear you are still my child, I'm the mom!! If I ask your ass what color is the sky you better damn well give me an answer. Do we understand each other?"
"What's going down here? I could hear you guys all the way in my room." Alonzo said while rushing down stairs to see what the loud voices were about.
"Oh no it's fine your sister here, little Ms. Kharma, thinks that because she pushed that baby out that she prone to her parents caring for her well-being but oh she has no idea."
Melita explained while making eye contact with Kharma who was also staring her eye to eye.
"You know mom, you are so sure that I left all because of Adam. Yea well for once you are wrong. In hindsight yes, I left because of him but in all honesty you were an all-around bitch

and I just couldn't take it. I do not see how dad or Alonzo dealt with it for this long." Kharma harshly said to her mother who was looking bewildered at her changed daughter.

"ALRIGHT KHARMA NOW THAT'S ENOUGH. YOUR MOTHER ONLY WANTS THE BEST FOR YOU AND I WILL NOT SIT HERE AND ALLOW YOU TO DISRESPECT HER ANY LONGER. NOW YOU WILL APOLOGIZE AND YOU WILL DO IT NOW!" Sebastian had enough of the feud between mother and daughter.

"No, no, honey. Let her have her moment" Melita told her husband.

"You know mom it seems like you are so worried that I will be a great mother, maybe even a better mother than you and it's killing you inside." Kharma teased at her mother in the most disrespectful tone.

"Little girl please, you see just because a dog has puppies that doesn't make it a mother understand?"

"Yea well that makes two of us doesn't it mother. Excuse me. Later Dad." Kharma left the table without finishing her food kissed her father goodbye and walked out slamming the door behind her. Melita and Sebastian sat in silence for a second both trying to figure where all this bottled anger come from within their daughter.

"Melita go after her she needs her mother right now," Sebastian suggested.

"She doesn't need me Sebastian you heard her she hates me and honestly I don't know why. I have loved and cared for Kharma since I brought her into this world and yet she acts as if I'm some wicked stepmother." Melita and Kharma both shared the same stubborn ways and it was clear to Sebastian. Melita went after her daughter as her husband requested, regardless of the nature she was still her only baby girl.

"Kharma wait! God come here baby girl," she reached her arms to wrap them around her hurting daughter. "What has that man done to you?"

"Mom, I'm so sorry I don't know where that came from." Kharma sobbed as she held on to her mother tightly. "He hurt me to my soul mom, and I feel like I'm going crazy."

"Look at me little girl, you are not going crazy sweetheart; you like any other woman fell for the wrong man and baby that's human nature. Life is what you put into it and baby girl you planted some bad seeds messing with that married man," Melita firmly said.

"Mom I realize that but I loved that man, I gave up everything for him and now I have this baby boy and it's like all the love I should have for him doesn't exist because I wasted it all on

Adam. It hurts mom to look at him, and I want to hold him so badly when he cries out for me but I can't. How? What mother does that?" Kharma searched for an answer in her mother's eyes and before Melita could answer her daughter a car horn sounded from behind them
Melita turned to stare at a very familiar face and she knew this meant nothing but trouble.

CHAPTER 3

(Four way Love Affair)

"Well aren't you two a sight, mother and daughter, whores of a feather must flock together or so I've heard," Lana Harris said in a shady tone.

"You know what this bitch done got on my last nerves." Kharma exclaimed while putting her hair in a bun and removing her sneakers.

"No, no baby I got this" Melita moved Kharma to the side where she could get a face to face view of Lana.

"Bitch I know you have more than enough sense to be driving up to my home talking shit to me, I guess all that money has clouded your way of thinking." Lana Harris smirked as Melita insulted her.

"Sweet and oh so innocent Melita Gomez. Tell me, did you tell your daughter about your high and not so holy days? You know what they say the apple doesn't fall too far from the tree," Lana hinted.

"Mother what is she talking about?" Kharma asked her mother out of curiosity.

"Nothing, see Lana here is like a parrot, no matter how many crackers you feed her she just won't shut the hell up." Melita clapped back at Lana.

"Yea and how many did my husband feed you huh Melita? What's the matter honey cat got your tongue!?" Lana spitefully asked a shocked Melita.

"Mom?!" Kharma called out

"You are such a damn liar Lana Harris!"

Just then Lana Harris pulled out a pair of black laced panties and tossed them at Melita Gomez who became lost for words. Kharma who had been waiting on an answer from her mother froze as well at the secret that started to reveal itself. Sebastian and Alonzo had been watching from the porch and decided to steer clear of the cat fight that was transpiring.

"Looks familiar Melita. If I'm not mistaken weren't you fucking my husband once upon a time? Oh wait that's right you forgot to mention that to baby girl over there."

"MOM, is this true, did you sleep with Adam Harris? MOM, did you or did you not sleep with Adam!" Kharma cried out for answers.

"YES, yes Kharma, but believe me sweetie it was before you and him were involved and I never meant for you to find out this way." Melita tried to explain to daughter.

"She's right Kharma it was 11 years ago." Sebastian finally decided to join in on the drama that was unfolding.
"Dad you knew about this too?" Kharma in disbelief asked her father.
"Mmmmm, Sebastian fine ass Gomez. Long time no see." Lana Harris boldly greeted Sebastian in front of his wife.
"Enough Lana, I think you need to leave our home now!"
"Now Sebastian, is that any way to talk to the mother of your child?" Lana exposed.
"LIES, LANA GET IN YOUR CAR AND LEAVE NOW. YOUR HOME IS BROKEN BUT THAT DOESN'T MEAN YOU CAN COME INTO MY SPACE AND WRECK MY FAMILY!" Melita got closer to Lana's face until they were nose to nose. Melita's face became flushed with anger at she stared down the homewrecker Kharma thought was just as innocent as a lonely house wife longing for attention.
"YOU BETTER GET OUT OF MY FACE MELITA. What you thought you could just come into my home, fuck my husband in our bed, and get away with it? Oh no that's not how the game of love goes. An eye for an eye, or in better terms, a nut for a nut," Lana mockingly stated.
Kharma was silent the entire time; she couldn't piece together the puzzle and all she wanted was to be out of it all.

"Sebastian, tell her. Tell your baby girl here that she is not your only daughter. Tell our young Kharma how you and I fucked on a rainy night; as a matter of fact it was the night after your mother over there fucked my husband."

"LYING BITCH!" Melita screamed as she slapped the wind out Lana. Lana's reaction wasn't what Melita had expected as she charged at her full speed ahead pushing Melita to the ground. Both ladies struggled to overcome the other as Alonzo laughed and looked on. Sebastian tried to break it up, while Kharma looked on as well shaking her head at the craziness of it all.

"SEBASTIAN GET THIS BITCH OFF ME!" Melita screamed out as Sebastian went to the aid of his wife.

"SEBASTIAN TELL HER. TELL HER THAT AIMEE IS NOT ADAM'S DAUGHTER, SHE'S YOURS!" Lana yelled out

"What. No I don't believe that!" Kharma said out of denial

"Yes Kharma, it's true Aimee doesn't belong to Adam; she is your sister, she is your father's daughter. We tried to keep you away from this; you and your brother, but you chose your own path and followed it." Melita tried to ease her distraught daughter's mind.

"NO no no no," Kharma repeated over and over.

"Sweetheart Just..."

"No, don't touch me. Do not ever touch me. As far as I'm concerned you are all hypocrites and I want nothing to do with this, not any of it." Kharma pleaded as she pulled away from her father's arms... She said her goodbyes to her brother who was just as shocked as she was at the events that had just taken place.

"And as for you Lana no I mean Mrs. Harris, ROT IN HELL!" Kharma made it clear to a very amused Lana who was not remorseful at anything she had done or caused at that very moment.

Melita cried in her husband's arms, as they watched their daughter walk away never looking back. Lana basked in her handy work then got into her car and jetted. Kharma thought the only thing there was to do was go back to Franklin and be the best damn mother she could be to her baby boy.

The events of that day continued to play in Kharma's head as she tried to shake them off. How could she live with knowing that her mother had fell for and made love to the same man she had given herself to. The thought of this made Kharma sick to her stomach. All this time her parents had so much to say about her personal life, yet they neglected to tell her their hidden secrets.

Just as Kharma was about to board the bus into town she caught glimpse of reality when Lana Harris pulled alongside of the bus and left her with a specific choice of words "Going somewhere Kharma, there's no need to run. I will be seeing you soon. Bank on it bitch." And with that Kharma thought that would be the last time she had to deal with Lana Harris. Things just seem to spiral so out of control all in a short period of time. Kharma had a specific game plan and it all went sour; so much for sweet revenge.

"Khar hey Khar wait, Where you going sis?" Alonzo had met his sister at the bus terminal and thought he'd get her to stay this time.

"Hey Lonzo what are you doing here. You know I can't stay not after what just happened with mom, dad, and Lana; this is too much. I have a son to love and I cannot do that bent on revenge; as far as I'm concern Lana has done enough for me and her." Kharma confided in her brother. He seemed to be the only one that understood her.

"Last call for all buses going south!" the bus driver announced over the PA system as he began listing all stops along the way.

"Franklin Tennessee" he announced.

"That's me well see ya around baby bro, and hey here buy yourself some new soccer shoes cause those things are worn out and don't be spending my money on none of these water for brain chicks you like to chase." Kharma laughed while hugging her brother goodbye. Alonzo watched the bus until it was out of site.

Kharma took in a deep breath and exhaled. All she wanted more than anything now was to get to her baby boy and hold him. Back in Aurora things seemed to go according to Lana Harris's plans. She gathered up some of her and the children belongings, as well as all of Adam's watches and what other valuables he kept in his office and made the long drive back to her parents' home to be with her babies.

While on the bus Kharma decided to phone Miss Carlene and Kristie and alert them of her return to Franklin.

"Hello Carlene here."

"Hey Miss Carlene its Kharma, listen I apologize for earlier I must have a bad reception or..."

"Or you just hung that phone on me child, that's alright I'm glad to hear from you, where are you?" Miss Carlene out of concern asked Kharma

"Miss Carlene so much has happened and I owe you and Kristie an apology and I am a bad mother this I know and

and..." Kharma could barely compose her words through the tears.

"And he misses his mommy, Listen child wipe those tears Kristie and Ka'Son will greet you." Miss Carlene assured Kharma.

The phone call ended and for the first time Kharma felt like her old self again and she couldn't wait to get home to her baby.

The bus finally pulled into Franklin, TN and as promised Kristie and Ka'Son was right there awaiting Kharma's arrival. Kharma caught sight of her baby boy and couldn't hold back any longer, she left her bags alongside of the bus and took her baby from Kristie's arms and for the first time she held him close to her heart. For the first time since the day he was born Kharma felt so much love in her heart for that little boy, not because he favored his father so much, but because he was hers all hers and no one not even Lana could change that or try to make a mess of something so right, so beautiful, and so meant to be.

The ride from the bus station was calm and relaxing. Kharma rode in the back seat with her baby boy and rested her head on the brand new car seat that Ka'Son slept so peacefully in. Kharma inhaled his scent of baby lotion and baby bath, a smell she hadn't paid very much attention to before. Kharma was bonding with her son for the very first time and from that day on she promised herself in silence that she would be a damn good mother and will never keep the truth from her son even if it may hurt him.

Upon pulling into the driveway Miss Carlene waved from her garden. She was excited to see Kharma; she hoped that for baby Ka'Son's sake Kharma had gained some clarity and in the sense of putting her child before any man.

"Grandmother, we're here. The ride put little K to sleep." Kristie alerted her grandmother.

"Well looks like my remedy worked. I tell you he is one fussy child but in a cute and cuddly sort of way." Miss Carlene smiled while helping the girls get the baby into the house without waking him.

"How was the ride?" Miss Carlene asked Kharma who was laying the baby
In his crib.

"It was comforting Miss Carlene and what I needed, some time to reflect. Some things were said and done while I was there in Aurora and I just would like to leave them where they belong. The day was almost over; Kharma had so much to vent over but it could wait until the morning. She had no idea that as much as she tried to prevent it Adam would still have this emotional control over her, even in her dreams...

"Kharma!" Adam's voice seem to call out to her in her sleep as she tossed and turned

"Kharma I love you!" the phantom cries just seem to get closer and closer as the images of a deceased Adam haunt her.

"NO, ADAM!" Kharma yelled out in terror, waking Kristie whose room was just across the way from hers.

"Kharma, Kharma wake up!" Kristie yelled out slapping a terrified Kharma who continued to sob uncontrollably.

"God, Kristie Adam's dead and it's my fault!" Kharma rocked back and forth as a speechless Kristie consoled her.

In the midst of it all Little K had woken up and needed to be changed and fed.

"It's okay Kharma I got him."

"No Kristie let me do this, it's long overdue."

Kharma removed the blouse that she was wearing and her bra. "Kristie could you give me one of the sanitary wipes over there and a wash cloth from my drawer?" Kristie knew why Kharma needed these things so after passing her what she asked for she excused herself from the room and closed the door behind her. Kharma after cleansing the area around her nipple gently picked her baby boy up and tried to get him to latch onto her breast for feeding.

"Come on baby latch on for mommy," Kharma warmly spoke to her baby boy.

Kharma knew it would be hard for him to breastfeed especially since she didn't take the time to actually bond with her baby boy in the first stages of him being born. Suddenly Kharma felt a suctioning feeling as she had looked away; she now turned to find her baby boy had latched onto her breast and began to feed. Kharma tried but the tears she could no longer keep. She was so excited she had to alert Miss Carlene and Kristie to the exciting news.

"MISS CARLENE, KRISTIE COME HERE HURRY UP!" Kharma called out to them.

"What, Kharma what's wrong are you okay, is it the baby?" Kristie came bursting in the door holding her cell phone in one hand and Miss Carlene was right behind with a Smith and Wesson pistol in her hands.

"What's going on in here?" Miss Carlene asked. The sight of these two ladies caused Kharma to laugh out so loudly.

"And what are you two going to do with that?" "Shit girl protect that baby and call 911," Kristie confirmed.

"Lord, no keep calm this is not that Kristie. Miss Carlene he latched, my baby boy knows who mommy is!" Kharma face lit up the entire room. Throughout her situation this was by far the best thing to ever happen to her and she refused to let anyone tell her anything different.

CHAPTER 4

(The Fugitive)

Meanwhile, back in Aurora the stench coming from the Mayor's mansion caused a concern neighbor to call the town's Sheriff's office.

"Hello, sheriff's department Kathy speaking," the dispatcher announced

"Yes, this is Mrs. Rooney over on Hemlock Lane. There is this foul odor coming from next door at Mayor Adam's house and well I'm just a little concern."

"Hi Mrs. Rooney, Yep well I'll alert the sheriff right away and he will get out there as soon as he can," Kathy assured the elderly woman.

"Hey Kat who was that?" Deputy Batemon asked while eating on a bagel.

"Same ole same ole. Mrs. Rooney wants y'all to come on out to the Mayor's mansion, she says it's a foul odor in the air out there and wants y'all to check it out."

"Ahhh that old lady is nosey is all and needs to worry about all those darn cats she has running around," Deputy Batemon clarified.

"Yes well it is your job so call up the sheriff and go, and I'm officially on my lunch break," Kat explained pushing the deputy out the door in a rush to get to the diner before the lunch rush.

The deputy dispatched Sheriff Simmons to the Mayor's mansion. He waited outside the home five minutes before going on ahead and checking out the property for himself. The neighbor who had called in was nowhere to be found which was typical in Aurora, people usually see and then they don't. Deputy pulled his pistol just in case there was an intruder on the property.

"MAYOR ADAM, MRS. HARRIS YOU GUYS HOME!" he called out but no responses followed.

He carefully approached the front door which he found unlocked causing even more concerns. Entering into the dead silenced house gave an uneasy feeling as he once more called out to the Mayor and yet no response. One thing that was much known was the odor that Mrs. Rooney had mentioned in her call earlier. He grabbed a cloth from his back pocket which he used to cover his nose and mouth. The smell of the death was very present in that house and it lead Deputy Batemon down the hall and into the master bedroom of the mansion where he discovered the body of Mayor Adam Harris covered with a brand new bed sheet and in blood.

"My God Mayor Adam Harris who on earth could have done this to you?" the young deputy asked himself.

"I'd better call this in." He goes back out to his patrol car and radio for the sheriff to hurry up and get there as soon as possible. Deputy Batemon soon calls in for the coroner to come and take a look at the body to gain insight.

"Yea sheriff you really ought to get over here looks like Mrs. Rooney was right about that smell."

"I'm just around the corner some nut job ran a stop sign and almost ran over a kid." Sheriff Simmons pulled up to the Mayor's mansion and was greeted by his deputy as well as the coroner.

"Sheriff," The coroner greeted him as he led him to the location of the body. Not sure how long he has been here, but judging from the nature of the body, I would say he has been here for at least a week," the coroner confirmed.

The sheriff pulled the sheet from the face of Adam Harris, and turned away after only one glance at the man who was once known as the most beloved mayor in West Virginia. The deputy began searching the children rooms, making sure that they hadn't met the same fate as their father. The only things that seem to be missing where some clothing items, along with the rest of the Harris family.

"Deputy Batemon, get on the phone and see if you can get in contact with Lana, let's see if her and those kids are at least safe and unharmed."

"You got it sheriff," before the deputy could follow orders there was a loud slamming of the front door which echoed throughout the halls of the mansion.

BOOM

"ADAMMM, BABY WE'RE HOME!" it was Lana Harris along with Adam Jr. and Aimee, their kids.

The sheriff signaled for the deputy to stop her before she had gotten far enough to see her dead husband's body.

"Hold on Mrs... Harris you may want to wait right here for a moment," Deputy Batemon suggested but Lana was not having it.

"No I will not and what are you all doing here in my house where is my husband?" Lana asked brushing past the deputy and continued down the hall

"Adam, what are the sheriff and ...OMG ADAM GET UP BABY WAKE UP! BABY TELL ME WHO DID THIS TO YOU? GOD BABY PLEASE WAKE UP!" Lana yelled out in tears. She dropped beside his riddled body and held his head in her lap. The children had heard their mother's cry and came running but was stopped in their tracks by the deputy who escorted them into the family room.

"Deputy Batemon is something wrong with our daddy. is he okay?" Aimee asked. She was old enough to understand but too young to see her father in that state.

"I want my daddy!" Little Adam pleaded with tears rolling down his face.

"Now I understand you kids are afraid and it's okay to be, but you have to trust me and stay put," the deputy consoled the worried children.

Mrs. Harris came storming past the door opening, her heels leaving marks in the floor.

"SHERIFF SIMMONS, I WANT YOU TO FIND THE PERSON WHO HAS DONE THIS TO MY HUSBAND!" Lana demanded; she was good at playing the grieving widow role which meant she had practiced for this very day. In all honesty she knew exactly who had done this and at the moment of leaving she spilled some very bitter tea.

Just as the coroner began giving the sheriff specifics on what he concluded had happened Lana Harris, the evil bitch that she was, decided to play God again and brought all darkness into the light.

"Excuse me sheriff, but I think I know who may have done this to my husband," she confessed.

"Is that right. Well hell who was it Lana? Speak up woman!" He demanded

"Kharma Gomez, Sheriff Simmons. She had this huge and sicken crush on Adam. She worked for us at the office but we had to fire her and she didn't take it lightly." Lana Harris put on a show so damn good even Adam from the grave believed the bull that was coming out of Lana's mouth.

"Kharma Gomez. Wait isn't that Sebastian Gomez's little girl?" The coroner asked bewildered at the thought of someone as kind as Kharma even committing such a crime. In fact the thought was sickening in the eyes of Deputy Batemon who has known Kharma since she was in grade school with this daughter.

"Sheriff maybe we should go by the Gomez's house just to check things out. For all we know Mrs. Harris could be just some scorned wife, how do we know she wasn't the one that...."

"Because I loved my husband that's why Batemon. Try to whisper a little louder so we can't hear you!" Lana interrupted Deputy Batemon.

"Look ma'am, this is normal procedure and until we have hard evidence right now you as well as Ms. Gomez are our number one suspects." Sheriff Simmons made clear.

"Guess that means I won't be taking my children to Disneyland now will I?" Lana sarcastically laughed, although the sheriff, deputy, and coroner had no smiles on their faces at all. The van had arrived to take the mayor's body away. The children were still in the family room so the coroner had ordered his assistants to carry the body out the back door and around to the van. As they followed orders, the driveway was now filled with nosey neighbors and news reporters.

"Damn it Deputy who in the hell let these people onto this property?!"

"I...I... I don't know sir I locked that gate once you arrived. Maybe one of the neighbors came in behind Mrs. Harris as she arrived and saw all of what was going on and spread the word." Deputy Batemon explained.

"Jesus Christ get those poor children out of here Deputy, take them around back get them in the car and wait there understood?"

"Yes sir."

"I'm warning you Deputy if any one of those kids faces end up on the 5 o'clock news that's your ass as well as your job, you got that?!"

"Yes sir."

Kids listen now Deputy is going to take you both to the car waiting outside while me and your mother talk to the nice people outside okay?" The sheriff assured the children trying not to seem too superficial.

"Okay now Mrs. Harris only tell them the minors, nothing major understood?"

"Yes sheriff by all means" Lana Harris agreed as she fixed her hair as if this would a great photo op. They slowly walked out the door as the cameras flashed and the uproar began.

"Now one at a time and I ask that you all respect Mrs. Harris's loss on today keep it short people." Sheriff Simmons firmly asked of the town's people.

"Mrs. Harris where you at home at the time of the mayor's demise?"

"No, our children and I were at my parents' house when I decided to come to check on my husband, after a few unanswered calls is when I learned of his death" Lana cried. "Does this have anything to do with the fact that Mayor Adam was in fact having an affair or the fact that Kacey Armani's body was found just a few weeks ago; is there any causes to believe that the two are somehow connected?" One bold reporter had her nerves of asking.
"Look folks it's been a long and hard day for Mrs. Harris and her children please would you all go home and leave her to mourn in peace." With Lana in tears the town's people felt sorrow for her and greeted her with their deepest sympathy.

After all of the commotion had gone away the deputy was ordered to take the children as well as Mrs. Harris in town to the station until further notice. Upon investigating the crime scene a little more Sheriff Simmons found what appeared to be the weapon used in the murder of Mayor Adam underneath the a pile of shoes in the far corner of the walk in closet. The smell of freshly fired bullets still lingered as he picked it up with a handkerchief and placed it into a plastic bag.

The house that had once served as the home front of one of the most beloved officials was now the center of a scandalous talk amongst the town's folk in Aurora. Lana had prompted the perfect crime and Kharma Gomez was the subject of yet another downfall which she had yet to learn about.

Knock

Knock

Knock

"Just a minute" Melita called out from the kitchen.

"Kharma honey I'm so glad you decided to come...back" Melita paused as she wondered why an out of town investigator and Sheriff Simmons were standing at her front door instead of her daughter.

"Ummm Sheriff Simmons may I ask to what do I owe this visit. Is it Alonzo? Is he and his friends disturbing the other customers down at the diner again?" She asked hoping that he'd say yes; besides the usual call ups the sheriff accompanied by an investigator spells something serious.

"Well ma'am we would like to talk to you about your daughter a Ms. Kharma Gomez. May we come in and have a sit down?" The investigator asked Melita's permission.

"I'm sorry sir and you are?"

"My apologies ma'am I'm Investigator Rowlands from Richmond. I am the one assigned to the Armani case and now...well let's just talk about this on the inside ma'am."

Investigator Rowlands was a tall man who stood about 6'3 and had a solid build, his skin was tanned and smooth and his eyes seem to be reddish brown as his eyes were the color of a dark green; he was a handsome man indeed in contrast to Sheriff Simmons, who was a short and stoutly built man. His stomach bulged over his belt buckle and his hairline was receding badly under his hat.

"Are you gentlemen hungry or thirsty? I have some sandwiches made and a fresh batch of lemonade I was making for my son and his friends, but you are more than welcome to have some." Melita's hospitality was more than warming but unfortunately the nature of these two law officials called for much more than some tasty lemonade.

"Now, what's this about and what does it have to do with my daughter?"

"Well Mrs. Gomez as you may or may not have heard Mayor Adam Harris was found dead in his home around 10 am this morning."

"Oh My God, SEBASTIAN GET DOWN HERE!" Melita cried out to her husband who was upstairs at the time.

"Melita you don't have to yell I can hear you." Sebastian inquired as he fixed his eyes on the two lawmen who sat in his living room.

"Peter what are you doing here with the sheriff?" Sebastian asked the investigator.

"You two know each other?"

"Know, Peter and I go way back, he was the quarterback and I was the wrestling champ at our old high school." Sebastian exclaimed to his wife as she watched the two men shake hands and hug each other in a brotherly way.

"So what brings you and our great sheriff here?"

"We'll have some disturbing news, I am afraid it involves your daughter; it seems like she is our prime suspect in the murder of Mayor Adam Harris."

"What, you want to run that by me again? Are you accusing my daughter, our daughter of killing that low life piece of shit Peter?" Sebastian firmly asked as his facial expression changed.

"Now hold up Sebastian!"

"NO, you hold up Sheriff, you waltz in here with your out of town lead Investigator over there and your Ivy League attitudes and start accusing my child of something so heinous. I want you to leave now!" Melita had heard enough Kharma may have made some bad choices but she was not a murder.

"But ma'am,"

"Sorry Sheriff, Peter, if the wife says it's time to go then it's time for you to go."

"Well I guess that's what it is." Not saying another word the two men made their way to the front door and saw themselves out. Tears filled Melita's eyes as she held on tightly to her husband.

"God Sebastian where is she? This could not have been our daughter's doing."

"I know let's just hope she is safe and sound wherever she is." Sebastian held on to his wife as they prayed for their daughter...

"Kharma, is it time to take the baby to the doctors yet?" Kristie called out to Kharma who was preparing to take Ka'Son to his six weeks checkup. She had a new lease on life and everything as far as Lana and Adam goes was now ancient history that is until she turned on the television set to record *The Young and The Restless* while she was away.

ALL POINTS BULLETIN

"In other news the search is on for this young woman shown here. Kharma Gomez is wanted in connections with Aurora, Virginia's late Mayor Adam Harris. Sheriff officials responded to a call early today that obtained a neighbor's complaint of a foul odor coming from the mansion in which Mayor Adam D. Harris shared with his wife and two children. The mayor's body was discovered by the town's sheriff and deputy, later Lana Harris the surviving widow, came home where she was questioned and gave her tip of what may have happened to the mayor. No funeral arrangements will be announced at this time."

The Breaking News ended as Kharma's face crossed thousands of TV screens in the Virginia and Tennessee area and maybe even further; at that moment Kharma's hopes for a new beginning suddenly went out the door, all in a split second.

"I think you have some explaining to do child." Kharma turned to find Miss Carlene standing behind her in a state of disbelief and shock. Kristie beside her dropped her head in guilt out of not telling her grandmother what Kharma had told her once before after having a nightmare about something and from the looks of it this is the reason why.

"Kharma, you all set we are going to be late for the baby's appointment," Kristie prompted.

"Yea let's go."

"Be back shortly grandma." Kristie kissed her grandmother on the cheek and headed to the car to help Kharma get the baby situated and strapped in.

"Kharma, like grandmother said it's time you start telling the truth, the entire truth," Kristie stated to Kharma as they pulled out of the drive way.

CHAPTER 5

(Fact vs Fiction)

The drive to the doctor's office was still and quiet. Ka'Son had fallen asleep easily from the drive. Kharma felt an uneasy feeling, as if time had stopped and stood still. She knew the questions would eventually start coming so she prepared herself emotionally and mentally for whatever Kristie would bring. To bypass the intensity of the drive, Kharma turned on the car radio being careful not to wake baby Ka'Son.

"I knew you were trouble when you walked in..."

The lyrics poured from the car speakers from Taylor's Swift hit song "Trouble",

quickly Kharma switched stations.

"Wait, hey I love that song why would you change it?" Kristie in her singing mode complained.

"Sorry, here I'll change it back."

"No actually turn it off we have at least five minutes before we arrive in town at the doctor's office and you are going to tell me something about what's going on."

"Kristie what are you talking about can't you just give it a rest"
Kharma became restless and all she wanted was to get the hell
out of that damn car.
Kristie who had become fed up with the merry go round of lies
with Kharma slammed on brakes.
"Jesus, you know, what is your problem Kristie?!" Kharma
scolded her while reaching in the back to check on her
sleeping baby boy.
"You, you are my problem. Here you show up out of nowhere
and my grandmother opens up her home to you. Okay that's
fine, but then you hide a pregnancy in which after you had the
baby you left, no more like abandon, leaving me and my
grandmother to care for *your son* while you go on some hell
bent spree of revenge and clarity. For days and weeks no
phone calls, no text messages,
and all of a sudden you show your ass back up and now you're
wanted for murder?!!"
"Oh God! You know what Kristie save me the soap opera scene
okay. I will gladly take my baby and we will leave in peace."
"There is no way you are taking that baby back there or
anywhere unless you tell me just what the hell it is you are
hiding, now talk!"

"Look! Kristie can we please get to the baby's appointment and afterwards I will tell you whatever you want to know okay." Kristie starting the car back up was a confirmation that she agreed to Kharma's terms...

They finally pulled into the parking lot of the clinic where it was hard as hell to find a parking space, but after two tries one was finally spotted closer to the entrance. It was windy out that day and the sun seemed to be going in and out of the clouds and the breeze smelled as if it were about to rain. The office was partially full of new mothers and some were even so lucky as to have the father of their child with them faithfully. Kharma sighed and glanced around as she wished for herself the same scene as she signed her baby in for his checkup.

The wait for those with appointments was not very long; after only five minutes of being there Kharma was finally called to the back.

"Ka'Son Gomez" the medical assistant called out from behind the opened door.

Kharma and Kristie gathered their things and carried baby Ka'Son to the back of the clinic where the assistant took his weight and vitals and all checked out very well.

"Well now this feller is a whopping 11 pounds 5 ounces!" the assistant revealed

"Good lord! Kristie what have you all been feeding him, look at him he is as round as a butterball turkey on Thanksgiving?" Kharma playfully asked Kristie

"Oh no do not blame us, it's all that breast milk you have been feeding him and he is a greedy ass baby too," Kristie replied.

"So I'll just leave this right here and the doctor will be in here very shortly."

"Okay thanks" Kharma couldn't believe how big her baby boy was getting she smiled at him as he made baby sounds and giggled after each and every one of them. He was a very healthy and happy little baby.

"Kharma, I'm still waiting on the truth."

"The truth about what?"

"Don't play stupid okay, you may have my granny fooled but it don't fly with me."

"Damn Kristie can't you shut up for once and worry about yourself!" Kharma was sick of the constant prying that Kristie was doing.

Kristie side eyed Kharma followed by her rolling her eyes.

"Knock, Knock Hi I'm Dr. Timonthy Stevens and how is this little guy?" The doctor greeted Kristie, Kharma, and little Ka'Son with a bright smile. He was about Adam Harris's height and build. He wasn't from around the area due to his northern accident. Kharma nor Kristie could take their eyes off of the doctor as they blushed over his honey brown eyes and his silken skin complexion which was a lighter shade of caramel, his hair laid wavy and perfectly trimmed.

"Kharma!"

"Yes Kristie I see him. Do you?" Kharma whispered back at Kristie

(Clears Throat) "Ladies, Hi nice to meet you, now which of you belongs to this bubbly baby over here? Hmm let's see if I can guess it correctly."

The doctor took a glance at Kristie and smiled and then quickly walked over to her "I knew it. Nice to meet you Ms. Gomez," he said as he turned towards Kharma, he had went over to her baby boy to pick him up to calm his now fussiness.

"How-how did you know?"

"Well it was no secret any blind man can see that little Ka'Son has his mother's pretty brown eyes as well as smile."

"Is that right Doctor?"

"As far as I can see yes ma'am."

"Ummm ok yeah so doc how long have you been a doctor here in Franklin?" Kristie intervened in on a possible chemistry that was about to take off way fast.

"Oh well for quite some time actually. I moved here from Washington to take care of my father, he passed with colon cancer a short time ago and I just decided to stay," he answered with swiftness. "Mmm hmmm and what about your family, is there a Mrs. Stevens? What about some mini Stevens, how many do you have calling you father?"

"Kristie!?"

"What! Listen let's just get back to the matter at hand doc," Kristie scolded

"Great, in that case Ms. Gomez if you would remove the baby's hat please I'd like to check his ears and cranial for closing soft spots just to make sure they are closing properly."

As the doctor did his duty with his patient Kharma eased away and thought she'd get the scoop on why the hell was she playing good cop bad cop with Dr. Stevens.

"What in the hell was that?"

"What was what?"

"Oh come on Kristie, don't act all innocent you were interrogating that man and you know it."

"Oh was that what I was doing? Honey I had no idea silly me."

"Don't get cute okay." Kristie humped her shoulders up as to brush off the suspicious findings Kharma called her out on.

"Alright well he looks good Ms. Gomez"

"Kharma"

"Pardon me?"

"My name it's Kharma, Dr. Stevens."

"Kharma, you have one healthy baby boy," he smiled. It was just something about this beautiful woman standing in front of him, something mysterious and hidden about her.

Her eyes seemed to stare into his and the world around them seem to disappear for a split second and in that second the love stricken doctor saw all the pain she tried to hide.

"Hellloooooo, Can we go now, Doc are you all finished up because I'm hungry and we do need to get this baby home," Kristie once more interrupted.

The doctor smiled "Yes of course. You guys are all set here. Just give this paper to my receptionist, and she will schedule an appointment for his first set of vaccines."

Kharma told herself that she wouldn't love another man but there was something different about Timothy Stevens. She knew he could see right through her, but for the sake of her heart and her son she decided to wipe the visions of this sexy ass doctor out of her head for good. She took the paper to the front desk as instructed as Kristie went out to settle Ka'Son into the car.

"Hi, and do you want a morning or evening appointment?"

"Oh umm it really doesn't matter as long as I can get in and out without such a long wait" Kharma replied with a smile as she caught glimpse of the charming doctor's phone number written on a blank piece of paper he had slide into the diaper bag while Kharma and Kristie talked and weren't noticing. The paper had been neatly folded and placed inside the pocket that held the baby's bottle Kharma noticed it when her arm brushed against it.

"Okay here you go you are all set to go," the receptionist passed Kharma an appointment card. While walking out of the clinic she caught glimpse of the doctor going into his office.

"See ya Kharma" he called out.

"Yeah, see ya Dr. Stevens."

Kristie shook at her head as Kharma entered into the car.

"What?"

"You are some piece of work you know that. I mean give yourself some time Kharma you just got your heart broken not to mention the no account bastard ended up dead and you my dear are the prime suspect."

"Kristie I don't need your history lessons okay. Besides he was checking me out and not the other way around."

"Whatever Kharma."

"Look would you just drop the freaking subject?!"

"Sure" Kristie agreed.

"God! You remind me of my best friend..." and right then Kharma paused for a second and a dead silence filled the car. "Your best friend who Kharma?" Kristie asked in a daring way. It was almost as if she challenged Kharma to finish her sentence.

"No-no one just drop it okay?"

"No let's not, Kharma you have some serious shit going on with you and this car is not moving another mile until you tell me just what the hell it is!"

Kristie had parked into the parking lot of a fast food restaurant and turned off the key in the ignition. Ka'Son was asleep in the car seat so they used soft voices to be careful to wake him.

"Fine you want answers?"

The man I fell in love with was killed. Did I do it?" I was there yes but that's all that was and that's all it ever will be so just leave it the hell alone. I'm trying to forget let me!"

"Fine geesh that's all you had to say." Kristie threw up her hands as a peace offering.

"While we are here we might as well get something to eat. Are you hungry?"

"Not really let's just get home I do need to lay Ka'Son down."

The rest of the way was more than just a drive, Kharma had received a text message from an unknown number. She clicked on the open message icon and giggled out loudly.

"Girl are you okay over there what you saw a naked man on that phone or what?"

"Not quite it's a message from Dr. Stevens actually, he wanted to make sure that we were okay and made it home safe and sound."

"Girl that man has got his eyes set on you and you better be careful cause a man like that is not some loner. I'm almost certain that there are some nurses at the office that get moist just from being around him all day."

"Eww you know if I hadn't been thinking clearly I would swear that you have a thing for Dr. McHotty as well."

"Me? Oh no he is hardly my type Kharma." Kristie laughed trying not to let Kharma see her blush.

He is every woman's type and Kristie was no exception. The clouds had gotten darker by the time they made it home.

"Get his bag. I'll get little Ka'Son" Kristie assured Kharma who looked tired. She struggled to get inside as the car seat and the diaper bag were both weighing her down.

"Kharma could you come in here for a second?" Miss Carlene called out from the living room where once again the news aired the information concerning Adam's murder.

"Miss Carlene I don't want to discuss this anymore Kristie interrogated me enough to and from the doctor's office; I just wanna eat, bathe, and touch my bed"

"Hush child nobody about to preach to you. What's done is done nothing more nothing less so let's just move on from that okay?"

"What I wanted to say was I am proud of you. You realized your wrongs and you came back to be a mother to that precious baby boy. I've seen the way you light up whenever you are holding him."

"Thanks Miss Carlene, I was so ashamed and lost without my baby I felt less of a woman, lower, and not at all like a mother."

There was nothing more farther from the truth. Kharma hugged Miss Carlene, kissed her goodnight, and went to join her baby boy who was sound asleep.

"I heard you and grandmother talking, Kharma she loves you a lot don't take that for granted." Kristie stepped from behind the bedroom door that belonged to Kharma.

"Wait, did you just come from behind that door and what you eavesdropping now?"

"Last time I checked I live here as well; you are merely a guest."

"What's your problem Kristie, listen is this about Dr. Stevens, you are more than welcome to have him." Kharma passed off as she got her things ready for her bath.

"You just don't get it do you and what's sad is that you never will.

CHAPTER 6

(Beautiful Stranger)

Kharma had a set of scented candles that aligned the nice sized bath tub. She calmly placed on some August Alsina and let the sounds flow through her ears as she began to think about the handsome doctor.

"I don't want nobody but you kissing on my tattoos"

"I don't want nobody but me talking to you until you fall asleep"

The lyrics sang out as she laid back and imagined herself somewhere far from everything and everyone. The music took her to a whole mother level as she became one with her body and for a moment's time she felt the touch of some familiar hands caressing her thighs underneath the steamy waters of the bath. She opened her eyes and in a frozen state watched as Adam sat right there on the side of the bath tub and smiled at her. There was something different about this smile.

This man was dead. "I saw Lana Shoot you" I-I"

"Shhhhhh" the vision she thought to be Adam had placed his finger up to his lips as she lay out a gentle moan when his phantom hands began to massage a very tender and familiar spot. Kharma threw her head back as she began to gasp and breathe heavier in pleasure.

Knock

Knock

"Kharma you okay in there girl. You been in there an awful long time!"

Kharma was startled at the sound of Miss Carlene knocking on the door. She glanced over to see that Adam had disappeared.

"Yea Miss Carlene I'll be right out I-I fell asleep."

"Well hurry and get out of that water we don't need you drowning."

"Yes ma'am."

"Kharma you are officially freaking out" she said to herself as she grabbed her towel and proceeded to exit out of the bath tub. She wrapped her towel around her soaked body and headed into her bedroom. Once there she found Kristie asleep lying across her bed and Ka'Son still sound asleep in his crib.

"Kristie, hey wake up go get in your own bed and let me get dressed in peace."

"Mmmmm, Just get dressed Kharma I am not trying to look at you besides you are not my type," a muzzled Kristie said.

Kharma smirked at the smart remark so she decided to call Kristie's bluff by dropping her towel and standing fully naked in front of her

"Kristie?"

"Hmm" Kristie peeked out of one eye and slightly lifted her head

"OMG EWWW I'M NO LESBO!" The sight of Kharma's nude body had awakened her for sure and she did as Kharma had asked of her first and foremost.

"Told you to get out my damn room" Kharma slickly said to her as she watched Kristie rush out her bedroom.

After getting dressed Kharma went into the kitchen to make her a salad but not before her phone began to ring.

"Hello, Kharma its Dr. Stevens."

"Oh well hi is there something wrong?"

F"Not quite, you see I have this young lady that has me thinking of her and for the life of me I cannot shake that feeling."

"What feeling is that Doctor, I mean you call my phone and you can't come out and say how you truly feel?"

"Please, Kharma call me Timothy and yes you're right, you must think I'm so kind of a creep calling your phone like this."

Kharma laughs in a seductive way "No not really, I actually think it's cute and yes I would love to."

"You would love to what?"

"Go on a date with you Timothy, isn't that what you wanted?"

The shy and bashful doctor laughed and replied with truth

"Yes, this is true it's exactly what I wanted Kharma."

"I knew it women's intuition," she bragged.

"Great, because we leave in 30mins I'll be waiting in the car."

"What wait-I" but he had already ended the call.

Kharma was so ecstatic about this she lost sight of the situation at hand.

"MISS CARLENE"

"I know this is last minute but can you watch Ka'Son for me, please?"

Miss Carlene could never say no to spending some extra time with Ka'Son so of course she agreed to do so when Kharma asked.

"Child you go ahead of me and Kristie would love to see you out and about and mingling."

"Speak for yourself grandmother, personally I think she needs to be here bonding with Ka'Son."

"That's exactly what I have been doing since I got here. Kristie why don't you go be miserable elsewhere."

That's cute Kharma you mean since you got back from chasing a dream oops I mean a man, who is now fucking dead. I think you need to rethink that statement if you think that for one second that you are just going to fall in love with that man, and abandon that little boy in there all over again you better rethink your priorities!"

"Wow okay I have no idea where all this is coming from Kristie but you may need to bring that tone down."

"Before what Kharma?!"

"HEY YOU TWO! Now that is enough Kristie you have no right to judge Kharma at all; she is well aware of what she has and hasn't done and as you can see she is trying to make her wrongs right so just stop it. All this bickering in front of this baby is something I won't have!"

Kharma agreed and stepped out of Kristie's face, finished getting dressed, and blew a kiss to baby boy before leaving for her date with Dr. Timonthy Stevens. Kristie returned to her bedroom to do some reading. She had just purchased a new Kindle fire and it was time to fill it up with great novels to read. Kharma thanked Miss Carlene once more and headed out the door to greet the patiently waiting doctor who had come to pick her up in a royal blue 2016 Dodge Charger.

"For a moment there I thought you may have forgotten little ole me out here."

Kharma laughed in a bashful way "No not at all I was sidetracked by some family issues if you can call it that."

"No need to explain; besides you find me a perfect family and I swear I would win the award for oldest adopted kid ever."

Dr. Stevens laughed at his own joke.

The doctor tried his best to make Kharma smile and it was working without fault as far as he could see. She seemed distant yet tense; he tried to figure out of a way to get her to relax so he thought to put on some music to ease her mind from whatever it was that was going on with her. Kharma felt a sudden wave of ease as the drive went smoothly she knew that he would began to ask questions so she prepared herself for the best of the worst. The music he had placed on was R&B and Soul, the first song would send a whirlwind of chills down Kharma's spine.

"New Edition Can You Stand the Rain" she said to herself.

"What do you need me to change it, is it not right for this occasion? Kharma just let me know to make you comfortable, and I swear, I would try my best to oblige you."

"No-no this is fine. I'm sorry if I seem so out of it. I have so much on my mind and it is getting the best of me," Kharma responded. What Timothy was doing was beyond sweet. If he knew of her past, would he run? She felt the need tell him the truth sooner than later.

"So Dr. Stevens, are you planning on getting married and you know having a family?"

Kharma side eyed him as to not to seem too personal and in his business. She expected him to either lie about it or avoid the question all together.

"To answer your questions no I have never been married. Have I thought about it yes numerous times and every time it seemed as if I have the right one it turns out to be disastrous."

"I didn't mean to pry I only wanted the truth. I have been through hell and back with a man who did nothing but lie and the entire time I believed every word,"

The ride had finally ended as the doctor and Kharma arrived at a small restaurant right outside of the city limits. Turning off the car Dr. Stevens turned to Kharma who had her head down with her hand resting covering half of her face as if she had a headache

Dr. Stevens was from the old school one thing he did not approve of is watching a women waddle in self-pity. "Kharma look at me." Kharma raises her head and looks. "None of what you have gone through is your fault. That man, whoever he was, seems to me wasn't a real man cause you wouldn't be sitting here with your head down now would you." "You're right. I am being so damn rude on this date with you." "No its fine Kharma just do me one favor." "And would that be?" "Have a good time with me tonight no worries and no issues, deal?" "Whatever you say Dr. Stevens," Kharma nodded. Once inside they were seated and even though Kharma had promised to remain calm, she couldn't help but pay close attention to how happy the other couples looked and all the laughter that filled the restaurant. The waiters were well dressed and they greeted each guest sincerely and warmly. Kharma felt as though she was a little under dressed with her all black leggings and v neck sweater dress on. She had pulled her hair back into a draping ponytail. "Hello, my name is Vaughn and I will be your waiter tonight can I interest you in a glass of our finest white wine?" "White wine, sounds expensive."

"Not at all, Vaughn in fact we will take a bottle on ice with two of your best wine glasses."

"Sounds great Dr. Stevens coming right up."

As the waiter walked away Kharma hesitated to ask Timothy just how Vaughn the waiter knew him well enough to call him by name.

"So is this where you bring all your women?"

"Is this you're M.O., you wine and dine them with white wine and fancy wine glasses? What's next? A 5 star meal which you don't mind paying for, and then what the nearest hotel?"

Timothy laughed despite how insulted he felt that Kharma would even think that he was the kinda man she was used to.

"That's it, are you finished reading me Kharma?"

"So you don't deny it, you what this date is over take me home to my baby Dr. Stevens."

Kharma got up from the table and began to storm off.

"Kharma, Hey wait what's wrong with you? I mean I have done nothing but treated you with the utmost respect and in return this what I get?"

Kharma had snatched away from the gently grip that Dr. Timothy had on her "Let go of me. You think you know me. You willing to face what I have going on with me!"

"What the hell do you think I have been trying to do since I said hello to you Kharma?"

"Look can we just go inside and enjoy ourselves?"

He held out his hand as Kharma took into it and they both walked into the restaurant as if nothing happened and gave it one last shot. Over dinner Kharma decided to open up to Timothy Stevens; she had a hard time trusting anyone but for some reasons she felt safe and at peace with this man.

"Here's your wine and glasses as you instructed Dr. Stevens."

"Would you like to order yet sir?"

"Yea just bring me the shrimp Alfredo and whatever the lady wants she gets," he signaled toward Kharma who was too busy reading the menu.

"Kharma?"

"Hmm, oh well I guess I'll have the same it sounds tasty, oh wait can we have a salad and some garlic and cheese breadsticks as well?"

"You got it ma'am."

"Thank you."

"I guess that lil chat we had rubbing off on you," Dr. Stevens smiled as he poured Kharma's wine for her.

"He was the mayor of our town in Aurora, Virginia. I fell for him something serious and I knew he was married but I allowed my emotions to overturn my thinking; long story short I ended up pregnant and here I am he didn't want the baby so I left."

"Kharma, No woman as smart and beautiful as you should have to carry that burden around and I'm sorry that you endured that."

"No need to apologize for another man's mistake it is not your job to do so."

"See that is where so many women go wrong, see real men apologize for the next man's mistake because in time you start to blame all of us."

"Can't argue with that."

They both laughed as their dinner had begun to arrive. The food smelled as good as it looked. Kharma had never had as much fun as she had that night with the Doctor. He kept her smiling from the first bite of food until the last drop of wine was gone. They shared stories of childhood silliness.

"It's getting late; I think we should call it a night. Let's get you home to that baby boy of yours."

"Okay, I really enjoyed myself tonight Timothy and I want to apologize for flipping out earlier."

"Hey, don't it's okay that's ancient history right?"

Kharma smiled "Yes."

"Good let's go."

The night ended with Kharma sharing so much laughter with a stranger to which she felt a connection with. Everything that came out this man's mouth was always so right in so many ways. He was so smart. He knew her fears and her desires within those few hours of being around her. Who was this man and who in the hell did he think he was coming in on his white horse like prince charming to save her.

"So I'll see you again right?"

"Sure."

"Kharma, its okay to feel wanted again."

"Who says I don't" she smiled closing the passenger side door. The doctor watched until he saw that she was safe and sound in the house and drove away.

"Miss Carlene, I'm home."

Walking up the stairs Kharma felt a sense of uneasiness. She hurried up to the stairs and into her bedroom she crept.

"What are you doing in my room?"

"Kharma, you scared me I didn't know you were home!"

"You didn't answer my question Kristie"

"I was just looking for my blue top but I realize you gave that back to me already,"

Kristie nervously brushed off.

"Kristie I doubt if you have ever given me anything to borrow of yours. I damn sure doubt that it would be stashed in my drawer where I keep all my important things."

"Again why the hell are you in here!"

"Like I told you I was looking for something that belonged to me but since I don't see it I'll go."

The two girls were once again face to face and this time Miss Carlene was nowhere to be found because she and Ka'Son were sound asleep in the next room.

If a show down would start it would just be those two going head to head.

"Yeah you do that Kristie go!"

Kristie went as she stated and slammed the door behind her. Kharma started to put her belongings back in order and soon after fell asleep.

The morning had come and the night had gone. The only thing Kharma could think about was how much fun she had the night before. She wondered if Dr. Stevens would call. Most of all she wondered what the hell Kristie was doing in her damn room rambling through her stuff. She had changed since Kharma had come back to be a mother to her son. It was a reason behind the actions Kristie was displaying.

"Good morning Ka'Son how's mommy's big man this morning."

"He's fine Kharma let's talk about the date you had last night with the steamy doctor."

"Eww Miss Carlene did you really just say that?"

Kharma giggled.

"Seriously it was great, I have never met such a more genuine man in my life. He didn't judge me after I told him about my past, all he saw was me. It felt good to know that real men still do exist Miss Carlene."

"Well child don't be so sure I mean you thought that mayor was the Prince of Wales and he turned out to be some ugly toad or what have you; yes girl everything that glitter is not golden underneath."

"She is clueless. Grandmother you are wasting your breath Kharma doesn't listen, remember how she went back after you told her not to?"

"Remember how I asked you to stay out of my damn room after I caught you snooping in it last night when I got home?"

Kharma insisted with a strong comeback.

"Kristie what were you doing in this girl's room?"

"Looking for my top and I told her ass that!"

"You told me after the fact and why you being disrespectful cursing in front of your grandmother?"

"Well isn't this nice from what you have told me this is sugar compared to the way you talk to your own mother but now you wanna come up in here and throw shade?!"

"KRISTIE THAT IS ENOUGH!"

"I'm not finished grandmother. She pretends to be Mary fucking sunshine. She is no different, she is fake and she is still a guest in our house she needs to learn that and remember as well!"

Kristie had such rage in her eyes for Kharma. She had almost turned into her enemy overnight.

"Listen, Kristie, I never tried to be anything nor anyone but my damn self. It's funny how you can dwell on my past but refuse to give me my props for at least coming home to my child. You have no idea how much I cry at night over the fact that I left him in the first place. I am well aware of my position in this house and until Miss Carlene says otherwise I am a part of this household and family just as must as you are so suck it up honey and back the hell off!" Kharma was done taking bullshit off of any and every one.

"This ends today, either you two find a way to co-exist in this house under the same roof or both of you will be out of here and on your own. Ka'Son would stay with me!" Miss Carlene declared. The two angry women both took what the woman of the house had to say very seriously and finished breakfast in peace and cold silence.

CHAPTER 7
(Say Goodbye)

After breakfast Kharma prepared herself Ka'Son for a day in town at the neighborhood's only park. She was in no way shape or form going to ask Kristie for a ride anywhere after the shit she has been pulling lately so she decided to call Dr. Timothy and ask him to join them as well.

Dr. Timothy

"Kharma Gomez"

"Timothy Stevens" her voice was so angelic to him

"Well I was going to take Ka'Son here to the park in town and I was wondering if you could give us a lift maybe even join us on this beautiful Saturday?"

"I don't why not, can you give me ummm 20mins and I will be there?"

"I'll be waiting doctor," the call ended and Kharma finished preparing.

Timothy had showed as promised and ahead of his set arrival time. Kharma wore a baby blue short sleeved dress with the latest fall boots and a small thin jacket wrapped around her waist. She decided to allow her hair to hang since the wind was not blowing that day.

"Look at you, looking good Miss Gomez."

"Thank you Timothy."

"No need to thank me for the truth."

Timothy was already earning the key to the kitty cat. Shit, it had been a while since Kharma had her cherry popped. You know how it goes, once that thang is ready it's ready and the doctor was causing emotions she never knew she had.

The park was very full that day. A puppet show had come to town and put on a show for the children.

"Wow this is interesting, look at how many people are actually here."

"Yeah the commission does this once a year for the kids, it's very fun and cool if you like these sorts of things,"

"Do you?"

"Do you like this sort of thing?"

"I would love it if I had kids of my own to attend it with every year."

Kharma smiled at the answers the doctor had given her. This man was either one helluva liar or he was being honest and at the very right moment. There was even a moment where she

caught glimpse of him staring at her and smiling. It was as if she had this kind of glow about her that he was drawn to.
"So I was thinking that maybe I could cook dinner for you and you can come over to my place tonight if that's not rushing things too fast?"
"No no I will be there just give me the time and directions."
"Not necessary, I will come and pick you up and we will go from there umm how does 8pm sound?"
"Sounds perfect Dr. Stevens"
The doctor flashed Kharma another smile as she made funny faces at Ka'Son who was bouncy in her lap while she holding him.
"There is no way in hell that I am about to pay no 5,000 dollars for no casket especially one for his trifling ass!"
Lana Harris sternly said to herself as she viewed some funeral and burial packages at the Smith's Funeral Home.
"A freaking rip off is what it is, Mother. I mean why I can't just toss his ass in a huge ass UPS box and deliver his ass to his mother and father let them bury him!"
"Now Lana! You know we did not raise you like this and you better respect the Lord and his work you know no matter how bad things may have been Adam would've buried you so damn nicely it would seem like your wedding day all over again."

"Mama that man that you are defending hurt me, how in the hell could I not hate him even in death?!"

"That man was the father of your children, he was not the greatest but he made sure whatever he was doing didn't make it to the door steps of the home he made for you and my grand babies."

"Mama, you have no idea and let's just leave it like it is and pick something so we could get out of here." Lana was not in the mood at all to be regretting the events of the cold and still figure she had once called her husband. Her mother always liked Adam; she was the kind of mother to give even the wrong doers the benefit of the doubt. What would she think if she knew that daughter who she had raised in a good God fearing home had become a widow by murdering her own husband in front of his side chick?

"Mrs. Harris did you find anything that is to your taste?" The funeral director questioned.

"As a matter of fact yes, that black one with the red padding would do just fine,"

"You-you sure ma'am I mean this is casket is for those of a no religious belief"

"What makes you think I believe in anything, besides it's appropriate for where he is going?"

"Fine ma'am you are the customer."

"Thank you."

Lana, wrote a check out to the funeral home and left. She would later find that Adam was better of a husband dead than he had ever been alive.

"Mother I need to go see my and Adam' lawyers to settle some important matters, I'll drop you at home with dad and the kids okay?"

"Okay you sure you don't need me to go along with you?"

"I'm positive I got this okay?"

"Alright baby well just drop me off at home"

Lana dropped her mother off as promised and headed out to the lawyer's office. On her way there she stopped to grab some coffee at the diner in town. The air was crisp and calm as she fixed her lipstick in her mirror and made sure her hair was on point before she got out of the car.

"Sebastian?" She called out as he was the first person she noticed when walking into the diner. He was well dressed and had just gotten a fresh shave it appeared. As he looked up he noticed a beautiful Bohemian with a mixture of Rican standing in all her glory at 5'4, Lana Harris. Her hands were nicely placed on her hips as she searched the diner for an empty table.

"Lana Harris, what brings you here?"

He motioned her to join him at his booth while he was enjoying his usual cheese omelet.

"I gotta have my caffeine you know that."

Sebastian smiled "Decaf, two sugars no cream a shot of vanilla right?"

Lana bit her bottom lip "That's right, I'm impressed you remembered."

"How could I forget?"

"Waitress?" He signaled

"Could you bring the lady here a decaf two sugars no cream a shot of vanilla."

"You got it sir" she wrote the order on her pad and went to prepare the coffee Sebastian Gomez had ordered for Lana.

"So, where's the little woman, I mean the wife?

"Come on Lana don't start, by the way I heard about Adam."

"What about him?"

"He was murdered woman don't you feel some kind of anger behind that if not any feelings at all?"

Lana changed the subject. "You and I had some wild nights or did you forget that?"

"Lana that was a long time ago and it was a mistake and I never want it to happen again."

"Don't be too sure love, you did say I was the best you have ever had, was that true or you just being a man trying to get an easy fuck?!"

"Listen, you really want to do this here shouldn't you be somewhere planning your husband's funeral?"

Lana changed her facial expression and body language after Sebastian had mentioned Adam once again. She could see that he truly loved his wife, if only she have had that same thing in Adam.

"Your coffee ma'am."

Lana thanked the server and stirred her coffee with a small red straw.

"Aimee needs to know,"

"Know what that the man that raised her, the man she grew to love, the man who has been there, was never her father. Really Lana do think this the perfect time to take her through all that?!"

"Sooner than later Sebastian. She is your daughter and after this thing with burying Adam is all over you will sit down with me and tell her!"

Lana, took two sips from the coffee gathered her purse to leave "You got this right, baby daddy?" She insulted Sebastian who in his view felt he was a damn good father and he had a point there is a time and place for everything and it was not yet a good time to tell Aimee Harris that she was in fact his.

As he watched Lana walk away he adjusted his tie. She had always had an ass on her that would bounce so nicely when she would walk away in anger.

"Lord have mercy" he said to himself as he snapped out of it and paid for his tab before heading to work.

The sign read "*Harper Phillip Law Firm*" as Lana pulled into the parking lot, she sat for a moment and said a prayer and proceeded to go in to meet with the lawyers about Adam's estate.

"Yes, how may I help you?" the receptionist politely greeted her.

Lana smiled back "Yes, Lana Harris here to see attorney Harper, I have an appointment."

"Ahh yes I see you here Mrs. Harris, have a seat and I'll alert him of your presence."

"No see that won't be necessary honey I can see myself into his office." Lana walked right past the receptionist "Hey! You can't go back there!" She yelled as she chased after her.

"Harper, who does this woman think she is talking to telling me to have a seat?"

"I'm sorry Mr. Harper I tried to stop her."

"No it's alright Nichole I can take it from here," the receptionist nodded as she closed the door to the office Lana had stormed in.

"Lana, you are a piece of work you know that?"

Lana locks the lawyer's office door and turned to face him with a grin as she walked over to him. "I missed you baby."

Lana sat on Harper's desk facing him with her legs spread and dress revealing some white panties underneath.

"Is that for me?"

"You know it boo," she sweetly uttered as he leaned in to kiss her; their sexual encounter was abruptly side tracked by a loud knock at the door.

Knock

Knock

Knock "Harper, it's Sebastian man open up I have some updates on that Fulton case."

Lana laughed as Harper struggled to hide his hard on she had caused before opening the door. "Hold on for a sec man,"

"Harper what the hell took you so long opening the door here I got the files that..." Sebastian paused at the sight of Lana Harris sitting so unbothered with a look deceit on her face.

"Like I was saying I got the files on the Fulton case man it's some serious shit in this pages. So look do you need me to take the case or what?" He asked Harper who seemed to have his hands full at that moment.

Harper looked back at Lana Harris before responding to Sebastian "Um yea, yes please man by all means that would me out a lot," Harper claimed.

"Nice seeing you again Sebastian," Lana called out in a sarcastic tone.

Sebastian flashed a smile and closed the door behind him. "What the hell was that all about with you and Sebastian?"

"What are you talking about?"

"Lana don't play dumb with me!" He came close to her as to intimidate her.

Lana was a bold bitch who never folded under pressure "Harper I saw the man in town that's all, now can we get to this meeting with Adam's attorney so I can get what I am owed?"

Lawyer Harper kissed her on the cheeks, gathered his briefcase and they both headed to the conference room. The meeting was short but intense for Lana who had to prove that Adam was being unfaithful the entire time. She presented solid evidence in a home video camera and letters from various women including one of which from Melita Gomez in which Lana never revealed her name. She also would show that she there was in fact a prenuptial agreement in which Adam signed meaning she gets control over his entire assets including money, bank accounts, cars; the list goes on and on. "Well if you would just sign these three forms. Mrs. Harris everything will be transferred into your name and your account within the next 48 hours," Adam's attorney explained. Lana looked at Harper as he gave her the okay to put her signature on the forms...

After Lana was done signing all the paperwork she decided to head home to be with her children. She kissed Harper goodbye as he walked her to her car.

Harper and Lana had been seeing each other since the day she found about him Melita Gomez. When she became pregnant because she was also seeing Sebastian at the time she secretly had a DNA test done with Harper and it had proven that he was not the father; she also had a test done with Sebastian Gomez, but the results showed to be 99.99%.

Walking back into the office Harper ran into Sebastian Gomez taking some files to his office. "Yo, Sebastian how do you happen to know Lana Harris is she like a friend of yours or something?"

"Why, man don't tell me you into her?"

"I may be inquiring."

"Dude she just lost her husband, give her some time to grieve."

"Seems to me she needs some comforting if you know what I mean."

Same ole Harper." Listen my daughter Kharma use to work for her and Adam in the mayor's office, but that's a story for the birds I'll catch up with you later man; I gotta get started on this case."

The two lawyers shook hands, all along walking away knowing that they have something in common other than being two of the best damn lawyers in West Virginia.

"Mom, it's me I'm on my way home everything went as planned I'll be home shortly after I stop at this store to grab a few things for dinner tonight." Lana spoke to her mother over the speakers of her car phone.

"Okay. I'll let the children know be sure to pick up some ice cream for them for after dinner."

"No, see that's why they don't listen to me now; you and dad continue to spoil them and it's making them rotten and stubborn."

"Yes, and make sure it's vanilla love you honey talk to you later," and with that the call ended with a beep.

"Always spoiling those damn kids," Lana quietly said to herself. As a child of money she never wanted for anything so she knew regardless of what she had to say her parents would give their grands the world. Lana's parents were good people with great hearts especially when it came to the grands. Though she wasn't always close to her father, she and her mother had this unbreakable bond; it was as if they were or could have been sisters. Dr. Sidney and Dr. Albert Malone had lived in Richmond Virginia way before Lana had been born, while working at the same Medical Clinic, but after retiring they moved to the outskirts of Aurora more like in the hills. Lana dropped her last maiden name of Malone when she was married to Adam Harris.

The trip to the grocery store didn't take long at all; there were no long lines so Lana was in and out. She then headed over to the newspaper office to give an official date, time, and place of her late husband's home going. It would be at 3pm Friday afternoon at the First Baptist Church. It was opened to the public as well as family, there would be no wake.

"I'm home kids!"

"Mommy, we missed you!" Aimee and Adam Jr. ran into their mother's arms and greeted her with hugs and kisses.

"You kids been good for grandma and grandpa?"

"Yes, Mommy, is Daddy with our gold fishy now?"

"Why on earth would he with your goldfish AJ?"

"Because Pa Pa said that he was now sleeping with the fishes."

"DAD!"

Albert Malone tried to avoid the look his daughter was giving him. "What, the boy needs to know the truth Lana."

Lana shook her head at her father careless teachings "Listen AJ; remember the story of baby Jesus. He needed a babysitter and well daddy was chosen so he had to leave to do his job; we don't want baby Jesus without someone to watch over him the way he watches over you now do we?"

AJ responded so innocently "No mommy."

"YOU'RE A LIAR!"

"Aimee!!"

Sidney ran after her granddaughter who seem to be upset and missing her father. Lana held on to AJ as she knew that while he had not a clue about death Aimee was old enough to know and realize that her father was gone and would not be coming back.

"Aimee sweetie, what is wrong with you yelling out at your mother like that?"

"I am sorry grandma but she act as if he is just going to walk through the door and everything is going to be okay."

"Understand me baby girl, she has to be weary of the fact that your brother is still very young and right now he just doesn't understand completely."

"I suppose you are right, I just really miss him he was my best friend and now he is gone forever."

Sidney gently rubbed Aimee's back "Not true at all, you see he is all around, as a matter of fact get up come over to this mirror."

"You see what I see?"

Aimee hung her head "It's just my reflection."

"Look closer."

Suddenly Aimee smiled "It's Daddy, he is a part of me!"

"That's right and never let go of that okay?"

Sidney hugged her granddaughter and she returned to the family room to apologize to her mother and baby brother; afterwards Lana and her mother prepared dinner and they all sat down and enjoyed their food on such a sad occasion.

CHAPTER 8
(Doctor of Love)

"Miss Carleneee, I need your help in here."

"Kharma, child look at you what on earth are you wearing a curtain?

Miss Carlene laughed at Kharma's attire she had chosen to wear on her second date with the fine ass Dr. Stevens.

"Tell you what, let me go in my closet and see what I have stashed from my young and feisty days."

Miss Carlene teased as she left to go into her closet to find Kharma something to wear that wasn't made in the 40's.

Just as Kharma was awaiting Miss Carlene's return Kristie made her way into Kharma's room "I could've had him too you know."

Kharma giggled "Sure, but you don't so why are we even on the subject again?"

"Kharma, you should never bite the hand that feeds you."

"I found it the perfect dress!"

Kristie frowned with envy, "Grandma you never told me you owned a small black cocktail dress."

"Well child of mine, that is only because you never gave me a reason to now have you?" Miss Carlene acknowledged Kharma laughed as she changed into the dress "OOOO sexy mama; go get your man girl!"

"Miss Carlene you are amazing, I love you, don't wait up." Kharma walks over to her baby boy who was sitting in his swing; he flashed a mouth full of gums. As his mommy kissed him goodbye as well "I love you too Ka'Son be good for Miss Carlene."

Kristie stood at her bedroom door "Bye!" Kharma bitterly said as she walked passed her and hurried down the stairs.

Once in the car, Dr. Stevens handed Kharma a dozen of pink long stem roses.

"Thank you sir how nice of you."

"Pretty flowers for a beautiful lady."

"You're looking neat and smelling good."

Timothy laughed at Kharma's compliment "Neat?"

"Yes, what's so funny?"

"Nothing darling," he mocked

"See this is starting off wrong already."

She gave him nudge with her elbow.

Timothy studied her "I must say Miss Gomez you looking extra neat yourself tonight."

Kharma glanced at him licking his lips as if he was admiring a piece of steak or something.

"Thank you!" she blushed.

The drive to Dr. Timothy's house was long and well worth the drive. "Here we are, home sweet home," he called out as they entered into the rock filled driveway leading up to his home. This man's house was huge, only an inch bigger and it would have been as big as the Mayor's mansion. Timothy got out and rushed to open Kharma's door for her.

"He is a gentleman as well, Kharma likes," she teased.

Turning the keys in the door he kindly told Kharma "Welcome to my man cave."

It was beautiful to be a bachelor's pad. His furniture was vintage and the paintings on the wall seem to be collector's items. The Victorian home had two main floors, and an attic, two bathrooms, four bedrooms; one of them a guest room. Kharma was giving herself a tour when the dinner bell sounded off "COME AND GET IT!" Timothy called out Kharma who was making her way down the stairs.

The table was perfectly set with real China and sterling silver utensils. There was a bottle of white wine on ice placed by the table and crystal wine glasses positioned at the side of each plate.

Timothy watched as Kharma made her way to the dining room area.

Pulling her chair out he observed the way she sat down "Do you always do things so beautifully?"

"I try not to trust me," she replied trying not to sound so conceited.

Timothy rushed off into the kitchen to begin serving the dinner he had made.

"Madam your dinner is served."

"Oh nice accent" Kharma laughed bashfully.

"Thank you and I present to you T-bone steak with a baked potatoes topped with bacon bits and sour cream, along with some cocktail shrimp on the side there, and for dessert you will have a double chocolate cake topped with whipped cream and a slice of pineapple."

Kharma was amused and turned on at the trouble this man was going through to make this night all about her.

"I am once more impressed doctor, that you went through all this trouble for lil ole me."

"Trust me you deserve it and to be honest I wish you'd let me be the one to whole heartedly give it to you."

Timothy was very serious and he had hoped that Kharma could see just how serious he was and that he was speaking from his heart.

The moon began to shine brighter as they laughed and at one moment Kharma even cried at the dinner table. The things that she had looked for or what she thought she had in the man who had broken her, she could now see it in this man who only wants to truly love her and care for her and Ka'Son. "Amazing that was delicious, I am full; you can throw down in that kitchen, where'd you learn to cook like that?"

"From my mother, when I was a little boy I use to come into the kitchen and add seasoning to the food when she would turn her back, it drove her crazy," Timothy reminisced.

"Well, she should be proud."

"If she were here I know she would be."

"I-I'm sorry I had no idea she was deceased."

Timothy placed his hand upon Kharma's "No it's okay I should have mentioned it to you."

"Here let me get these plates for you."

"Umm that's generous, but no I will do the dishes you are my special guest. You just have yourself a nice seat and I will be right back."

Kharma drunk her last swallow of wine, removed her red and black pumps, and made her way into the kitchen where Timothy was preparing the dishwasher for the dishes he carried into the kitchen with him.

After dinner had been served and the small talk mixed with sexual innuendos had ended Kharma could feel the aged wine he had served affecting her sexual hunger.

When he cleared the table and took the dishes to the kitchen sink she followed.

Kharma placed on some music for what was about to take place. As The Weekend's "Earned It" soared throughout the house Kharma continued on her mission to the kitchen.

As he stood at the sink, she wrapped her arms around him. When he turned around to face her, he stared into her seductive eyes. He leaned in and kissed her passionately. Kharma responded in a way that felt almost foreign to her; wanting, needing, and craving him.

He lifted her and carried her to the room while still leaning towards her lips, placing more kisses on them.

He gently laid her down on the bed and assured her that she would be okay. She smiled and nodded her head.

He began to undress her carefully removing each piece of her clothing, one piece at a time.

He unbuttoned his shirt showing his rippled chest and stomach. From the looks of it, he worked out when he was not at the hospital. She was impressed when he removed his pants and she saw the bulge of his dick protruding from the bottom of his boxers, which he was now taking off.
He reached into his wallet and applied the prophylactic to his manhood.
He knelt down before her and began to kiss her inner thighs making his way to moisture of her love box.
"May I?" He sensually asked Kharma as he could tell her heart beat had begun to speed up.
"Yesss" Kharma whispered. Her legs had already begun to quiver at the thought of this man kissing and licking on her clit. After receiving the okay Timothy went for the ultimate climax with Kharma. He began flickering his tongue over her clit as he gently slid his finger in and out of her now well moist pussy.
"Yesss, Shit Dr. Stevens your tongue feels so damn good. Oh my god!"
"I want you to do me a favor sexy. I want you to cum for me and do not move when you are ready to do so. Cum for Dr. Stevens beauty!"

Kharma nodded in agreeance of what Timothy demanded. Temperatures began to rise as started to lick her pussy faster and faster "Cum for me baby," he whispered over and over to her.

"Mmmmmm, Timothy I'm cumming baby oh my god I-I-I" and before she could say another word all of her sweet juices poured into Timothy's mouth causing him to become even more aroused.

"Timothy, I want you inside of me so bad" she couldn't control her emotions anymore at this point.

Timothy climbed on top her and wrapped her legs around his waist once more. He lifted her placing her head on his shoulder and without warning began to fuck her while standing and holding her in midair. Kharma moaned out in pleasure as he balanced her up and down on his dick.

"You like that beautiful?"

"Fuck, Timothy yes faster don't stop deeper harder!" She ordered him as he fulfilled each and every need of hers. He gently eased her back down on the bed while turning her on her stomach he placed his hand under her and lifted her slightly arching her back and entering inside of her from behind.

"Damn, girl you're wet!"

He licked his lips and began to long stroke her from the back doggy style. Kharma was no rookie as she began to throw it back on Timothy's larger manhood.

"Shit Kharma! That's it beauty work that pussy for me baby."

Kharma, cried out even more "FUCK DR. STEVENS I'm CUMMING!"

Speeding up with her he himself was about to bust "Cum baby cum, you can do it? Cum all over this dick!"

"OOOOO FUCK GIRL I'M CUMMING WITH YOU!" Timothy cried out as he firmed his grip on Kharma.

Kharma collapsed onto the bed; ass no longer in the air, arched back gone. Timothy kissed her booty cheeks and held out his hands to her.

"Kharma come with me," he asked of her so sweetly.

"Where are we going?"

"You trust me right?"

She nervously nodded a yes as he led her down the hallway to the master bathroom.

Upon entering Kharma became speechless at the view.

"Timothy, What-what is this?"

"It's for you, something I feel like you deserve."

He removed the silk black sheet that she had wrapped around herself and guided her into the large round bathtub *that was filled with a bubble bath with pink rose petals floating above the water.*

At that moment a single tear drop started to roll down Kharma's cheek, but before it could drop from her face Timothy placed his hands underneath her chin and caught her tear in the palm of his hand.

"Look at me baby, no more tears. I am here now and I will worry for you I will cry your tears for you; most importantly I want you to know and understand no one will ever hurt you again. I love you Kharma Gomez as well as that handsome son of yours."

"Love me? You don't even know me Timothy." Kharma pulled away.

Timothy held on to her "Look at me, Let me be the judge of that, for now we about to take a nice bath together and whatever happens beyond that is totally up to you."

She smiled; she had already made love to him so what else was there to give very but her heart and soul.

CHAPTER 9

(The Black Widow)

Friday couldn't have come soon enough for Lana Harris. She was up early getting her and the children's attire ready for the funeral of their father. She had purchased a brand new bed and sheets to put into the bedroom she once shared with her husband. As loving as she may seem at one point of time in life, her heart was now as cold as the ground she was about to place her late husband in.

"Harper wake up, you have to go before the kids and my parents wake up!"

Harper rolled over grunting and holding on to Lana as he smiled while still sleep.

"Harper!"

Lana shoved him off of her.

"Damn Lana what's the problem with you this morning woman?!"

He angrily said as he sat up in the bed.

"You have to go I told you that we discuss this over the phone"

"Uh huh and was that after or before you I licked that chocolate kitty cat of yours baby?"

Lana smiled at his clap back game.

"Look that's cute but seriously get your clothes on and go, you know I'm burying Adam today."

"Adam?"

"Damn Lana you announcing him like he's some everyday Tom Dick and Harry."

"Yep, and let's just hope you don't get that lucky."

"Lucky, shit who said I wanted to marry you?"

Lana gave Harper a look of "nigga what?" She wasn't at all an ugly bitch. She was around 5'4 with a chocolate complexion. She had a mixture of Bohemian and Rican in her which explained her nice waist line and her ample but perfectly round ass that sat out just right whenever she wore form fitting clothes. Her skin was smooth and beautiful, but her personality was not to be toyed with. Her parents had always taught her that the higher the self-esteem the higher the results. Just because Harper was lawyer did not mean he was an exception to that rule.

Harper got his things and was out of there being careful not to wake anyone in the mansion.

"Harper I love you" she called out.

"Fuck you Lana. Oh wait I just did."

Lana gave him an even more devilish look as he turned and continued out the front door.

By this time the sun had come up and it seems. Everyone in the Harris household was up and about.

"Lana can I talk with you for a moment?" Sidney peered into AJ's room where she was grooming his hair

"Yes, mom what is it?"

"Aimee told me she heard you last night talking to someone in your bedroom. Girl don't you have no other man in you and your husband's home already that's bad karma."

"Now, see right there is when I end this conversation."

"Don't you walk away from me Marie!" Lana paused she knew that the only time her mother calls her by her middle name was or if she is angry with her.

"Mom, Aimee is an eleven year child mourning her father, her best friend of course, and she thinks she's hearing a man's voice at night."

"You may be right, but then she maybe a child whose mother has moved on already."

Lana, stared as her mother she walked away. She had to be more careful next time.

Things were more at peace in the Gomez house hold. Melita had gotten up to cook a nice breakfast and press Alonzo and Sebastian's collar shirts for the funeral of Adam Harris.

"Dad, why do we have to go again I mean I honestly didn't know the man like that?"

"Lonzo, go set the table for your mother and yes you have to go. Regardless of what may have happened with him and your sister he was still the mayor of this town and as citizens and out of respect we owe it Lana to at least show up and show our condolences."

Melita, stopped what she was doing to correct her husband on one thing.

"Clearly we don't owe Lana ass shit but an ass kicking!"

"Sweetheart come on don't start this now okay?"

"Start what? You need to be worrying about your daughter but I guess you could if you would just keep your eyes off Lana's ass!"

"Well mom you have to admit she does have a nice future behind her." Alonzo came to his father's defense.

Melita looked at Sebastian and then her son again, "Okay so she has a nice ass I admit it but I still don't like that stuck up heffa."

"Son what about her breast though?"

"Okay see now you are pushing it!" Melita playfully chased her husband around the house with a wooden spoon.

(Jonathan calls an Old friend)

"Hello?"

"Kharma are you coming to Adam's funeral?"

"Jonathan, why are you even calling me, I thought I paid you to shut up?"

"Well yeah but don't you realize by now I couldn't stop talking to you if I tried."

Kharma smiled, "Same ole Jonathan Short."

"Sort of" he replied in a displeasing tone.

"To answer your question no I'm not coming and do not call me again unless it's something serious going on with my parents!"

Kharma ended the phone call on a sour note. The nerve of Jonathan of all people, asking her presence at Adam's funeral; Lana would cause a big scene and the law would be after her for sure.

"You should go, isn't that what you wanted Kharma to see Adam pay for what he did to you?"

Kharma rolled her eyes at Kristie who had been standing at her doorway listening to the entire conversation she had with Jonathan concerning Adam's death

"Do you know the meaning of the words "knock first?"

"Do you know the meaning of the words "you are just a guest here?"

Kharma rose from the spot where she was sitting on her bed and walked slowly towards Kristie

Once near her she held her ear a lil closer to Kristie's mouth

"Now, tell me while I am closer so I can get the picture."

Just as Kristie opened her bold ass mouth Kharma closed it for her

Slap

Whack whack

"GRANDMA, GET HER OFF!"

"STUPID MISERABLE BITCH I HAVE HAD IT WITH YOU UNDERSTAND ME?!!"

"GET OFF ME YOU PSYCHO!"

"KHARMA, KRISTIE. STOP THIS, STOP IT NOW!"

Miss Carlene tried her best to pull these two girls apart but Kharma had grip on her so strong it would take more than Jesus Christ himself to separate her hands from Kristie's hair.

Finally by some miracle she loosened up and let go.

"Miss Carlene that is it I can no longer live here Kristie has made it clear that she does not want me here and as far as I am concerned this is her home not mine nor Ka'Son's.

"Kharma don't you dare think about taking that baby away from the only home he has ever known, listen you are just upset, you both are."

"No! I am sorry grandmother but she needs to go and make sure you take that spoiled ass baby of yours with you."

"BITCH WHAT?!!" Kharma yelled while charging into Kristie once more this time knocking her ass to the floor. Kristie was able to squirm away from Kharma this time once free she ran into her bedroom and locked the door.

Kharma went after her banging on her door to gain entrance "What's wrong Kristie you got all that damn mouth, unlock the damn door. What you afraid of me now huh? You weren't afraid when you were talking shit!"

Kristie didn't respond back as Kharma turned and walked back into their own room to pack her and Ka'Son's belongings, but not before she made one very important phone call.

Can I stay with you?

"Timothy, did I catch you at work?"

"No, I am actually off on Fridays, what's wrong are you okay?"

"I had a fight with Kristie, this is so embarrassing."

"Kharma, say what's on your mind baby."

"Can Ka'Son and I live with you until I find a place of my own?"

"That's it, that's the question that has you all nervous?"

"Yes it is Timothy understand I do not like asking people for help of any kind."

"That all changes right now, so get packed and I will be over in like 15 mins, do you need a moving truck?"

"No, I came here with little, and I'm leaving here with even lesser"

Timothy ended the call with a "See ya soon."

"Kharma!"

"Not now Miss Carlene, This has been in the making since the day I stepped foot in this house. I adore you for what you have done for me and my baby I honestly do, and will forever be grateful but I have to go."

"No, you don't have to Kharma when you are going to stop running? Honey as long as you run your problem swill never be solved."

"That's just a risk I am willingly to take."

Beep

Beep

"I'm sorry Miss Carlene, Thanks for everything I love you."

Kharma sealed her goodbye with a kiss and headed out. After Timothy had helped her with her bags and aided her in placing Ka'Son in his car seat and strapping it down she took one last glimpse of the house she had grown to love and waved goodbye to
the sweet elderly woman who had given a roof over her and her son's head.

"Tsk, I'm glad that's over, finally some peace and quiet" Kristie stood in the driveway beside her grandmother with her arms folded.

Miss Carlene looked her granddaughter with disbelief and hurt "Kristie Armani I have never in my life been so angry at you the way I am now, I swear you act more and more like Kacey everyday it's no wonder your mother handed you over to me."

Kristie stood in silence as she watched her grandmother walk into the house slamming the door behind her.

"So, do you care to talk about it?"

"Not really Timothy"

"Are you sure I mean I suck at listening but I will do my best."

"Timothy,"

"Oh come on Kharma things couldn't have been that bad."

"TIMOTHY!"

Kharma blurted out "I said No, let's just get to your house okay?"

"As you wish." Timothy felt a sense of hurt and confusion. Here this beautiful woman had laid with him and now she decided to push him away.

"Okay, here we are once again. You already know where everything is at so you can pick a bedroom and get comfortable"

"Timothy, I want to apologize for earlier in the car you know snapping at you like that."

"Hey, it's no problem we all have our days right?"

"Let me go get your bags and bring them in."

Kharma started up the staircase with Ka'Son in her arms. And began peering into each room finally she had made her choice she knew Timothy would agree with it indeed.

"Kharma did you find which room you ..." Timothy paused and stopped in his tracks and smiled brightly at the sight of Kharma standing in the middle of the master bedroom hold baby Ka'Son smiling back at him. The light of the room gave off halo over her and had never looked so beautiful.

"I see you have made your choice, and you know what I wouldn't have picked a better choice myself "He leaned in and kissed her as well as placing a kiss on Ka'Son's forehead "Welcome home" he concluded.

"Lana, the family car is here." Sidney alerted her daughter who was putting the finishing touches on her assemble.

"Marie!!"

"What is it now mom?"

"Don't play stank with me girl you are not considering wearing an all red dress to your dead husband's funeral service?!"

"Mom, how can I consider when I am already looking damn good in it."

"Don't use that tongue with me Lana Marie, I swear you are as cold as ice."

"Mmmm Hmmmmm and as hot as fire, now can we get going, it's hot in this dress and I want to get this over with, so I can change into something I can move around in."

Sidney looked at her daughter and said no more.

"Wait, Mom does these red bottom heels go with my dress?"

Sidney gave Lana that "child of mine make me slap you" look before getting into the family car.

CHAPTER 10
(Love vs Lies)

"Grandmother, I don't think I want to see daddy in that box."
"Oh, Aimee it's not a box honey and trust me it's very pretty
your mother and I picked it out ourselves."
"Really, is it pink?!"
Sidney laughed pulling her granddaughter closer to her "Not
quite Aimee, you will see once we get there for now I want you
to brace your young mind for what is about to come to pass on
this day of home going okay?"
"If there is anything you don't understand please baby you
hold on as tight as you can to me."
"Okay" Aimee rested her head on the arms of her
grandmother and grew silent. She peered over at her little
brother who was sitting in Grandpa Albert's lap afraid of the
big strange car.
Lana was of course in neither, she had decided to drive her
own car to the services as she noticed Harper behind her and
the Gomez's behind him. She sent Sebastian a quick text
thanking him for coming to Adam's funeral.

Melita dropped her head in disappointment and snatched her husband's phone

"Give me that! Really we are in a funeral line and why isn't she in the family car with the family and why is she sending text messages?!"

"Babe, why are you asking me it's not like I have the answers to that Lana has never let anything or anyone get her down," Sebastian preached.

"I guess," Melita testified.

Kharma watched on as she witness the hundred something car funeral line on TV. The local news station in Aurora had covered the story since day one. She felt a sense of sorrow. She looked over at a giggling and bouncing Ka'Son who was busy bouncing in his brand new bouncer and sing along Timothy had

just bought him. She saw Adam but she also saw herself in him.

Kharma quickly turned the television set off as she heard Timothy come into the house she quickly wiped the tears away

"Honey, I'm home," he called out jokingly.

Kharma went to greet him "Oooooo what's in the box?"

"Hmmmm. Why I don't know what is in this strange box that I am carrying."

"Timothy stop playing what's in the box?"

"What box?"

"That box"

"This box?"

"Timothy?!"

Kharma managed to grab it, it was kind of heavy but when she unwrapped it she was amazed to find that it was in fact an Affenpinscher. Her coat was all black and freshly groomed. She was wearing a collar that read "Evita" she was very frisky and active.

"Oh my god baby, you got us a doggy?"

"Um. No I got you a dog"

"Timothy she is beautiful!"

"That makes two of you now doesn't it?"

Kharma placed Evita on the floor "So what you calling me a female dog now?!"

Timothy looked at her curiously "No baby I was just saying that..."

Kharma interrupted him "Gotcha!" she laughed at her prank moment.

"So what was that you were watching on TV before I came in?"

"Oh just some news nothing exciting"

"Great well, I am going to put this dog food away and you my sweaty Kharma are going to relax upstairs in a nice hot bubble bath while Ka'Son and I do the manly thing."

"And just what is the manly thing?"

"Oh back to back episodes of *Uncle Grandpa* on the cartoon network channel."

"OK well that is my exit signal you two play nice I will take Evita with me."

Kharma picked up the small dog and went to have her me time.

"The organ began to play as a Soprano voiced choir member sang out throughout the church "His Eyes Is on The Sparrow" The church was nice and big. The choir wore robes of royal blue and white. The pastor had been Adam's pastor as a small child.

Lana and her children walked hand in hand as her parents and Adam's parents followed.

Once everyone was seated the pallbearers brought in the all black casket that contained Adam's remains.

There was not one dry eye in the entire church and as cold as Lana may have proclaimed to be she was sobbing hysterically so much so that for a minute there you would almost believe that she actually miss her husband. The pastor began his sermon with reading scriptures from the Old Testament of the bible. Many *"Amen* and *Yes Lord!"* filled the atmosphere in the church.

"Daddy!"

"Aimee ran up to Adam's casket and begged him to wake up."

"Daddy wake up, you promised you promised you would never leave us, Daddy please!"

"Lana, go get your daughter and hold her!!"

"Mama she is looking for attention!"

Suddenly without any warning or second thought Sebastian Gomez got up from his seat with his wife and son and walked slowly where Aimee and her grandmother was, kneeling beside Adam's casket. Sebastian wrapped his arms. Around Aimee picked her up and carried her back to his seat holding on to her as she wept. For the remainder of the service Aimee stayed positioned in Sebastian's lap as she finally calmed down enough to return to her seat beside her grandmother and mother. Melita felt the need to go right over to Lana Harris and slap the shit out of her but she refused to do so in front of those children.

Soon the service was over and was to the grave site from there.

"Ashes to Ashes Dust to Dust," these were the pastor's final words.

Walking arm in arm with his wife Lana approached Sebastian "Thank you, what you did was nothing short of amazing, not many men would have done that."

"You mean like your boyfriend over there Harper?"

"Sad, what real mother and wife brings their side man to their husband's funeral Lana?!"

Lana smirked at Melita's side comment, "Sebastian get your hound before I make this heffa sit like a good bitch."

"What skank?!!"

Melita charged towards Lana as Sebastian held her back "Like I was saying that was real sweet of you for what you did for Aimee."

"It's called being a father Lana, we gotta go!"

Lana shrugged. As his parents walked away Alonzo had a few words to add to the situation

"Biiiiiiiiiyyyyyyaaatttchhhh!" He exclaimed in slow motion

He then turn to walk off but not before he ask one more thing of Lana Harris

"Nah, for real can I have your number?"

"Pffft!!"

Lana stormed off at the insult Alonzo had just made.

"Lana Marie Malone Harris, girl I have nothing to say to you."

"God! Mama don't start not now okay?"

"Last time I checked she was your mother not the other way around Lana."

Lana turned her head in the direction of Alina Harris, Adam's mother.

"I'm sorry, I could have sworn this was between me and mother Alina!"

"Let me tell, you something you weren't crazy enough to disrespect me when my son was alive and you damn sure will not start now!"

"Alina, today is not the day okay. Adam was and will always be my husband and like I told you when he was here, like it or not I am still and will always be his wife!!"

Alina sneered her nose up at Lana "Puff his wife? Than act like it!"

Alina and Adam D Harris II walked peacefully to their limo and disappeared off into the distances.

"Come on y'all let's get out of here before Adam himself decide to rise up and voice and irrelevant opinion." Lana was the last to leave the grave site placing a single red rose on her deceased husband's casket.

Once everyone was out of clear view and sight someone who would have been very familiar to Adam walked up the paved road and into the graveyard. Stopping to check her surroundings she proceeded to move closer to the casket that held Adam Harris. As she reached the burial spot she placed both the palms of her hands on the lid of the casket and laid her head upon it as well, "Baby, can you hear me? I swear whoever did this to you will regret this shit and more. Sleep in peace I love you!" and without another word being said the stranger turned and as quickly as she had shown up she was gone.

"Kharma, you okay in their baby?"

"Yea love just meditating I'll be out in a sec."

"Alright."

Kharma, tried not to think about what she had seen on the news earlier yet she just couldn't shake it. When Ka'Son had gotten older what would she tell him if the subject ever arose about his real father?

Evita her brand new puppy began to bark all of a sudden as she tried to quiet her Timothy came through the door wearing nothing but his stethoscope around his neck carrying some fresh strawberries and a can of caramel whipping cream.

"Mmmmm, I guess I have been a good girl to deserve my very own man dessert, but then I don't want to spoil my appetite doctor."

Timothy held out his hand and helped her out the bath "Wait
where is Ka'Son is?"

"Did I ever tell you that I have an aunt who lives just up the
road there?"

"No, you kinda forgot that part."

"Well now you know and trust me she is very good with
children so you have nothing to worry about okay. Kharma do
you trust me?"

"Yes baby I do."

"Now can you tell me why?"

Timothy stopped her words from leaving her lips by placing a
single finger on her lips. "Shhhhh, follow me beauty."

Hand in hand they reached the bedroom area which had
scented candles lit all around it Kharma was not used to
something like this. She felt sort of guilty, here was this
amazing man treating her like more than a queen and she was
too busy mourning over Adam's doggish ass; it wasn't fair to
her and it damn wasn't fair to Timothy.

Kharma laid back on the big soft beautiful bed.

Timothy kneeled as he parted her thighs.

"Isn't she beautiful baby?"

*"Shhhhh" he instructed her as he gently parted her lips as if
he was handling something breakable.*

Timothy began to kiss her from the bottom...slowly up.

"Oh my God!"

"mmmm" he hums on her pussy

He licks slowly down

"Timothy damn baby!"

"Shhhh!"

He takes her legs and puts them on his shoulders.

After he lifts her ass off the bed and puts her pussy to his face
and sticks his tongue in...licking it slowly.

Kharma holds on to him tightly "baby oh my god, don't stop!"

Timothy smiles as he nibbles on her clit while licking her up
and down.

"Fuck!" She exclaims in pleasure.

He starts licking her clit quicker as she let her arms fall and
she lets her body form with his and began to suck his dick
while he is licking her.

He places her on her back and without warning began
fucking her holding her tightly and intimately.

"Doc-doc- Dr. Stevens fuck!"

"And whose pussy is this?"

"Yours Doctor!"

"Whose?"

"oooo shit, Yours Doctor!"

They shared the most passionate kiss in the midst of this session they had long forgotten about the strawberries and whipped topping.

"Dare me Baby"

"I dare you," Timothy uttered

and with that Kharma came all over his hardened dick. Timothy held her closer as he himself came.

"Dr. Stevens, what am I going to do with you?"

"Let's see; love me, trust me, fuck me."

Kharma softly punched him on his arm "Seriously?"

"I am being serious, you do that and I am one happy man." He slaps her on the ass "Now come on let's get cleaned up so we can go get Ka'Son."

Kharma would soon find that her peace she had found in a world full of noise would soon come to an end by the person once trusted.

On their way to pick up Ka'Son she had this feeling that something just wasn't right.

"Timothy, after we go to pick up Ka'Son I'm thinking about calling my mother here to visit for a few days if it's okay with you?"

"Sure, I have no problem with that."

"Good, thanks."

"No need for all that she is the woman who birthed you into this world to be honest I need to thank her for having you," Timothy sincerely expressed.

Kharma leaned over and kissed him on the cheek.

"I love you too."

"Wait, did you just say the L word?"

"Is that a problem Kharma?"

Kharma smiled "No cause you know what I love you too."

The rest of the day was silent. Kharma was in the room reading to Ka'Son and Timothy had gone out to purchase a new doggy bed for Evita. Once asleep Kharma laid her baby boy in his brand new baby crib and sat down to call her mother.

"Mother it's me how are you guys?"

"Kharma, it would have been nice of you to at least bring that baby to his father's funeral."

"Really mom you knew as well as I did that Lana would've had me arrested and don't try and tell me differently, I know you've heard and seen this on the news."

"We may have heard parts of the story."

"Listen I called because I wanted to know if you would like to come visit me and Ka'Son, and mend this craziness between us like daddy asked?"

"Well I can do that Kharma you know that."

"When you are done packing go to the bus station and pick up the ticket that I am sending you and when you arrive I will be waiting for you."

"You got it baby girl!"

"Thank you mom I love you."

"I love you too Kharma."

"Who was that sweetie?"

"That was our daughter, Sebastian baby"

"She wants me to come see her and our grandson."

"Why only you?"

"She says she wants to mend things up with us."

"Sounds good to me."

"Sebastian there is something wrong; I know my daughter."

"Well when you make it to her just asked her. Don't force it, just ease it out her."

"You are right."

Later that evening Melita did as Kharma had asked of her. She arrived at in Franklin,TN and just as she had stated Kharma was there waiting on her mother with Ka'Son and Timothy Stevens.

Kharma hugged her mother tighter than she had ever before.

"Mom, thank you so much for coming!"

"Kharma regardless of what you and I go through I will always be there for you."

"I know."

"Now is this my beautiful grandbaby?"

"Yes it is his name is Ka'Son."

"Oh, and mom this is Dr. Timothy Stevens."

"It's pleasure to meet the woman who is responsible for this beautiful angel right here."

"Flattering isn't he, nice to meet you as well doctor and from the smile on her face I can tell you are keeping my daughter very happy."

"That's my job, come on let's get you ladies and baby out this night air."

"So Kharma, you know that evil heffa Lana Harris showed up to her own husband's funeral wearing an all red dress with some red bottom pumps and to add gasoline to the already large fire she invited her lover as well."

"Wow, you know mom can we talk about this later I'm kind of tired"

"Well all I'm saying is you could've brought the baby to his father's funeral."

At that moment Kharma dropped her head as Timothy looked her with surprised eyes.

Melita, who had caught sight of that quickly silenced her big mouth.

"Okay mom welcome home as I always tell family the guest room is right next to the baby's room, make yourself at home." Melita obliged as she took a sleeping Ka'Son to lay him in his crib.

"Um, Kharma can I speak with you for a moment?"

"What's wrong?"

"Just what happened so bad in Aurora that you ended up here in Franklin, cause your mother seemed damn happy to see you and even more excited to see Ka'Son. Is this her first time seeing him?"

Kharma knew how bad it would hurt her to lie to this man whom she claims to love.

"Listen, The funeral my mother was speaking of was that of my son's father. He was the mayor, Adam D Harris III, he was married I use to work for him and we ended up having an affair behind his wife's back in which I became pregnant by him. He didn't want me nor Ka'Son so he paid me off to leave and I did. After ending up here in Franklin I met Kristie and Miss Carlene, they opened up their homes to me. I had had the baby but I was so screwed up I went on this revenge

rampage; things went wrong some people ended up hurt and
now Adam is dead."

"Did you do it?"

"Timothy"

"Baby, did you kill Mayor Adam?"

"I was there and that's all I can tell you; just trust me okay
Timothy?"

Kharma grabbed him by his shirt as he started to walk off

"Baby, trust me okay?"

She pleaded while kissing him.

CHAPTER 11

(Differences)

"Mom, Are you awake I want you to meet Miss Carlene and her granddaughter Kristie."

"Kharma, you do not have to yell and yes I am and dressed as well as Ka'Son"

"Well let's get a move on, Miss Carlene cooked breakfast."

"I'm coming, no need to rush."

Melita carried Ka'Son in one arm and his diaper bag in the other

Kharma laughed" Mama you look like you are carrying Alonzo on your hip all over again."

"Girl do not remind me, your brother was a lazy baby who refused to walk even though he could."

"I remember and dad use to make him walk by holding a snickers above his face. Now look at him all grown up slim and fit and pretty; soon he will make me an aunt."

The two laughed as they hadn't noticed that whatever was broken was now slowly mending itself.

"You lovely ladies ready to go?"

Timothy held the door opened for them like the man he was.

"Kristie, did you set the table?"

"Yes Grandma, do I have to be here? I mean honestly I rather go watch golf on TV."

"Kristie stop whining and go get that honey and sit it out for me, thank you."

Kristie was not into the fact that Kharma was bringing her mother over to introduce her. She figured as much as she dislikes Kharma she may feel the same about mother.

"Grandma they're here!"

Miss Carlene stood out front to greet them as Kristie stayed behind in the

house.

Kharma jumped out the car and ran up to hug Miss Carlene

"Dang Kharma girl you knock me and you to the ground. I missed you too."

"Hold on I want you to meet someone."

Melita exited the car with Ka'Son in her arms. "Nice to meet you Miss Carlene, I wanna thank you for taking my daughter and grandson in and under your wings."

"Oh, honey don't mention it."

"I'm Melita Gomez by the way and it's an honor to meet you."

Timothy waved as he had gotten out to retrieve their bags.
"Well hello there Miss Carlene I hear you cooked up some of
that famous breakfast of yours."
"You know it come on in this house and get you some."
Now Miss Carlene, I'm here with Kharma."
Miss Carlene caught on to the joke and gave Timothy a shove
on the arm "Oh no I couldn't keep up with you if I tried but
that does not mean I will not try," she laughed.
Upon entering the house and sitting down at the breakfast
table Kharma noticed Kristie was already seated at the table.
"Oh hi Kharma, I didn't realize you were coming over and look
you even brought more guest; Hi Dr. Timothy!"
"Nice to see you again too Kristie."
"Hmph likewise."
Miss Carlene cleared her throat to excuse her granddaughter's
rudeness "Kristie this is Melita Gomez, Kharma's mother"
Kristie glanced over at Melita who was smiling and holding
out her hand to shake with Kristie."
"Hi!"
Melita gave Kharma a look of "No this lil bitch didn't."
Kharma gestured for her mother to brush it off.
"So Miss Carlene how long have you been living here in
Franklin?"

"Well Melita all my life actually, my daughter she had some problems and soon it went from me living me alone to raising Kristie over there."

"Grandmother!"

"Kristie is there a problem?"

"Why are you telling strangers our family business, it's none of their business!"

"Who are you calling me a stranger though Kristie?"

"Was anyone talking to Kharma because I sure in the hell wasn't?"

"Mama could you go place Ka'Son in his swing and turn on the rocking sensor?" Melita did just that.

"Miss Carlene you may have to excuse my language."

"Bitch let me tell you something, Miss Carlene invited us here to her yes HER home for a meet and greet breakfast, now until she tells us otherwise shut the hell up and grow up!"

Timothy intercepted "Miss Carlene this looks great can we all pray and eat?!"

"Sure Doc I'll feed you"

"I'm sorry Kristie I don't eat spoiled meats they tend to sour my stomach."

Kristie got up from the table and stormed off upstairs to eat her food in the privacy of her own room.

"Melita you will have to look over Kristie, lately I have no idea what's been on her mind."

"It's okay Miss Carlene I have a daughter and believe me it's a ride I have to take with caution daily."

The two grandmothers laughed as they connected in many ways.

After breakfast Kharma gave her mother a tour of the house she had once lived in.

"And this was once me and Ka'Son's room and as you can see it is still how I left it."

"Kharma can we have a seat on the patio, we need to talk you and I."

"Sure mom let's go."

Timothy was in the front watching TV with Ka'Son and Miss Carlene went to have a talk with Kristie.

It was a sunny day, the warmth of the sun warmed the cooled patio

"Kharma I know that you and I have never seen eye to eye, but..."

Kharma stopped her mother "Wait mom I refuse to sit here and allow you to sit here and take all the blame for something that I allowed. You are my only mother if something happens to you I will feel like I have just lost my soul. I apologize for all the disrespect and the anger I showed toward you. Listen I love you thank you for never giving up on me and no matter what you are always there for me no matter how far I push you away."

"Kharma girl, you are my only daughter come here."
Melita and Kharma both in tears, exchanged a joyful mother and daughter moment.

"Kristie what is wrong with you this morning child?"
"Grandmother it's Kharma. Why is she acting like she is so perfect when she is not and you seem to have forgotten how she just up and left her baby boy; you and I had to care for him and not once did she express how grateful she is."

"Thank you Kristie!"
Kharma had been standing in the doorway the entire time; she had heard every word.

"I'm grateful beyond that even. I don't understand why you see me as a sworn enemy when we were the best of friends once."

"You are right and I do apologize for the way I acted with your mother where she is so that I can apologize to her?"

"She's out on the patio, she has grown to love it out there."
Kristie walked past Kharma and went to join Melita out on the patio.

"Mrs. Gomez I just want to apologize for earlier I have been going through so much lately. I miss my mom and sister and I just felt like Kharma came to take my spot."

Melita motioned for her to have a seat "Kristie listen I understand, Kharma isn't like that though she is a genuine person at heart."

"Yes ma'am."

Timothy came out into the garden where Kharma was smelling some freshly grown roses that Miss Carlene had planted for her.

"A pretty flower for a beautiful lady."

"Hey you what are you doing out here?"

Timothy wrapped his arms around Kharma's waist placing his face into her neck "Mmm you smell as good as these flowers."

Kharma turns to kiss him "I love you too. Hey let's get out of here, I'm kinda tired."

"Okay, you get Mom and I'll get Ka'Son situated into the car."

"Mom, are you ready, we are about to head out."

"Oh, okay let's say goodbye to Miss Carlene."

"Miss Carlene we are about to get home, looks like it's about to rain."

"Well it was a pleasure meeting you Melita and you be sure to come back anytime."

The clouds began to roll in as they traveled back home. There was a mere moment of silence. Timothy was focused on the road, Kharma was focused on Timothy, and Melita was too busy adoring her grandson.

"Lana, where's Aimee?"

"I don't know Mom and I am tired of chasing that child!"

"She has lost her father Lana Marie; most importantly she is your daughter, she needs you more than anything right now!"

"Look, I have to go get some things from the office check in her bedroom Mom."

"I did she isn't there."

"Sidney I found her she's in here!"

Albert Malone called out to his wife from Adam's study. When they got there Aimee was seated at her father's desk and had fallen asleep with her head rested upon his desk in her hand she held on tightly to his tie.

Lana walked over to her sleeping child and tried to wake her up without upsetting her any more than she already was.

"Aimee, baby come on let's get you in the bed."

"Hmm Daddy?"

She was calling out for her father in her sleep Lana looked over at her parents.

"No sweetie it's mommy come on now you can't sleep in here."

"N-N-No, I want daddy!" Aimee snatched away from her mother and ran into the arms of her grandmother, who carried her down the hall to her bedroom while trying to comfort her.

"I swear dad it's like she hates me, more like blames me, for what happened to her father."

"Nah, I just think she misses him a lot; she will get over it soon just be patient with her."

Sidney returned to the family room where AJ was playing with his legos.

"She's asleep."

"Lana, you may have to get this child some help with coping with the loss of her father."

"Mom there is nothing wrong with Aimee she needs to stop acting like a baby!"

"Baby or not get that child some help!"

"Fine look I am late can I go now?"

"Gone on get out of here."

Sidney placed her hands on her hips as she watched her cold hearted daughter walk out the front door, Gucci Bag in hand.

"Martin hey boo I am on my way to you as we speak"

"As always Lana it is going to be a pleasure doing business with you, see you in a bit."

Lana blows kisses through the phone as she hangs up. When she arrived at the bank she forgot her ID in the car so in a hurry she ran out to get it. Not watching what she was doing she bumped into Sebastian Gomez once more.

"Lana, why am I not surprised to see you here?"

"Because, I'm all about my coins boo and this is after all a bank"

Sebastian gazed upon her chest as her V neck blouse revealed her perfect breast.

Lana saw what he was adoring and used it to her advantage "You like those huh, but then that wouldn't be anything new now would it?"

"Do not flatter yourself Lana"

"Trust me I wouldn't dream of doing that, when are you going come see Aimee?"

"I will not do this not here and if you think for one second that I am going to come to your home you are sadly mistaken."

"Yeah you're right; I need a man not a man who's too wrapped around his master's, I mean his wife's finger now if you will excuse me I have a check to pick up."

CHAPTER 12

(Fu$% you...Pay Me)

Lana walked into the office of senior banker Martin T. Edwards. She was a well-known customer of his.

"Hey baby cakes!" he greeted her kissing her on both cheeks.

"Please tell me you have some good news for me Martin."

"You know I do Mrs. Lana you received a deposit yesterday in the sum of five hundred thousand dollars!"

Lana was stunned as she held her heart "Are you serious Martin?!"

"As a heart attack; it seems that Adam also had some stocks as well as other valuables."

"When he died you became the sole keeper of it."

"That bastard wasn't shit when he was alive but in death he has taken care of me and our children for the rest of our lives."

"Well I just need your signature and you will be all set"

Lana did as she was instructed and placed her name on all the important documents.

"Now, cut me my check sweetie."

"Check, girl you better place it in your account."

"Oh Martin you are too cute, but I got this."

The banker shrugged and gave in to Lana's request.

"Dad where did mom go?"

"She went to see your sister and your nephew son."

"I don't understand why she didn't want all us to come."

"This is one of those times where she and your mother need to bond son, sort like what you and I do when I take to the golf court with me."

Alonzo frowned "Dad that is not the same, carrying your clubs as well as your buddies is not what I call bonding."

Sebastian raised his eyebrow "But I taught you how to golf son."

"Big deal I could've taught myself."

"You met that nice server at the country club."

Alonzo stopped in his tracks "Well, okay you got me on that one."

"Let's just hope when your mother comes home she's in great spirits with Kharma."

"Yeah let's, look dad I would love to chat but I told Jonathan that I would go to the store with him to pick up some things for this party he is having later on tonight."

"Party? Jonathan Short's party?"

"Dad come on what is the problem?"

"Nothing son enjoy yourself as long as you don't mention it to your mother you know how she feels about that young man."

"You got it dad, thanks see ya later."

Beep

Beep

Beep "Hey Alonzo come on man we gotta beat this sale!"

"Man like I'm right here I heard you the first time!"

Once in the car Alonzo noticed that Jonathan tried to avoid the subject of Kharma.

"So, heard from your sister lately?" He plainly asked Alonzo

"Nah man I haven't why, you miss her or something."

"You don't?"

"Kharma was the light of my life you know that Lonzo. I been trying to get with her for years with not much success."

Alonzo agreed "Lame dudes tend to fight for her attention."

"So wait bro are you saying I'm lame?"

"No you just said it and now I'm cosigning; you are lame as hell bro."

They both laughed.

Later that day in Franklin, Kharma lay peacefully in Timothy's lap as he played in her hair. Melita had taken Ka'Son downstairs into the living room to watch some cartoons while she did some cleaning.

"Baby, what's on your mind you have been so silent since we have made it back home. Is it me, have I done anything wrong?"

Kharma lifted her head from his lap "No, you have done everything so right, I just never want it to end."

He places his finger underneath her chin, "Beauty as long as you continue to love me I will return that love in abundance."

The bond between these two were unbreakable and Kharma knew for sure that this time it was real. She kissed him and drifted off to sleep in his lap. Once asleep, Timothy carried her in his arms upstairs to the bedroom and placed her under the sheets.

Kissing her on the forehead he whispered into her ears "I love you."

"Mmmmm I love you too baby," she called out from her sleep.

"Melita, how are things going down here did we leave you enough to do?"

"Plenty, good thing Ka'Son is occupied with those cartoons I would never get any of this done."

"Yea he keeps me and Kharma busy but I love him as my own."

"That I can tell Timothy and that is why I salute you. Not many men would be willingly to take in another man's baby."

"Well mama Melita I think you will find that I am not many men, I am me."

Melita smiled, "of course you are now get out of my way, get..."she flagged the broom at his feet running him out the living room.

"When Kharma awakes tell her I had to run to the office for something I will be returning shortly."

Melita waved her hand without looking up "Okay bye."

"Harper can I drop by or do you have some skank in your house, is that the reason why you twice sent me straight to voicemail?"

"Lana, Last time we talked, you were kicking me out of your home."

"Be a man, you knew our agreement and there is no way you are coming around my children yet, they just lost their father remember?"

"Oh wait you care, I mean really care cause from where I was positioned seems to me you didn't give a flying fuck about Adam or his home."

"Look I don't need a moment of clarity, what I need to know is do you want this fee I owe you for being my attorney cause I can keep my coins in my pocket?"

"Yes just come through I'll leave the door unlock for you."

"Knowing his ass he better not have some other tramp up in there when I get there.

Lana pulled into the gated house where the successful attorney lived. His car was partially parked in the two door garage and as promised the door had been left opened for her. His home was on point for a man's taste. Lana smiled as she made her way to Harper's bedroom. She crept down the hall to find Harper patiently waiting on her with nothing but his boxers briefs on.

"And what do I owe this honor Mr... Harper?"

"I just get excited when you are around as you can see"

Lana licked her lips "Oh I see alright and as tempting as it looks I am here on a business call, nothing more; now take this money I have some more important things to handle."

Harper counted it. "Is it all here?"

"Fuck you Harper!"

Lana turned to leave she felt insulted.

Things in Aurora were about to take a turn for the worst. Things that once were will be no more. Though she and her daughter had patches things up it could've not come at a more vulnerable time. While Kharma was in Franklin playing house with the doctor, Sheriff Simmons and Investigator Rowlands were putting together an arrest team. They had been notified by someone very close to Kharma that she was in fact living in Franklin, TN.

Lies will become the truth and Kharma Gomez will once more be at the mercy of Lana Harris.

The day Kharma Gomez lost her freedom would be also be the day that reality hit's hard in the small town of Aurora.

Monday morning Timothy had gotten up and ready for work as he normally did. Kharma was still asleep and Melita was as well. Ka'Son had just fallen asleep right before Kharma drifted off.

"See you later beauty." Timothy kissed Kharma goodbye and made his way out the door. The day began as a normal week day, school buses were running on time and were all filled with kids. As the first bus zoomed by the house Timothy unlocked his car door. The slam of the door woke Kharma; something seemed off to her so she quickly gathered up Ka'Son and went into her mother's room.

"Mom, Mom wake up I need you to do something for me."

"Kharma, girl it 7am in the morning what is it?" Melita asked in a groggy voice
I need you to take Ka'Son back to Aurora with you and I want you to look after him okay?"
Melita looked confused and bewildered "Kharma sweetie, you are scaring me what is going on!?"
"Mother! Just tell me you will, please?"
Melita could see the fear in her daughter's eyes "Okay of course I will."
Just as Timothy had pulled off for work his car became surrounded by Franklin squad cars.
Timothy had a look of wonder on his face.

Kharma's Arrest

Police: You, sir drop your keys out of the window and hands on the dashboard
Timothy tosses his keys out the window "Alright officer just don't shoot."
Police: Place both your hands on the dashboard.
Timothy slowly did as he was instructed. The officers then rushed up to the car and asked him to exit the car. Once more he did as he was told.
Once out of the car he could see that they did not come alone.
"Sir is there anyone else in that house?"

"Sheriff I don't think I am obligated to tell you that."

"Son you will tell me, and I will walk into your home via the door or I will have the door kicked down causing major damage."

"Good thing I make enough money right so getting the kicked down door fixed should be easy."

The sheriff and investigator gave the okay for the swat to kick the door in and standing right there was Kharma Gomez. In all her boldness she stood proudly

"SIR SHE'S RIGHT HERE!"

One of the arresting officers informed the sheriff.

Sheriff Simmons walked up to Kharma and without looking her directly in the face to avoid seeing her tears he began to ask her various questions like did she know Adam Harris, and did she understand why she was being apprehended.

With a blank stare she kept her eyes on Timothy who was just as in shock as she was.

"Kharma Gomez you have the right to remain silent anything you say can and will be used against you in the court of law. You have a right to an attorney if you cannot afford one, one will be appointed for you."

"Kharma, do you understand your rights that have been read to you?"

Kharma looked at the arresting officer who was placing handcuffs on her and nodded yes. She turned to the sheriff, "Sheriff Simmons I have one question. How did you know I was here?"

It was then that Kristie stepped in clear view and made her presence known.

Kharma's heart dropped into her stomach as Kristie stood there in her face enjoying this moment.

Without warning Kristie positioned herself beside Kharma "That's for my sister bitch," she whispered softly in Kharma's ear. Kharma's eyes filled with tears as she finally received the answer to the burning question of why Kristie hated her so much all of a sudden. "Ms. Armani thanks for your help and cooperation."

"You are more than welcomed sheriff."

"Sorry about your sister Kacey she was a fine young woman," the sheriff implied as Kharma looked on. As they brought her outside she turned away to keep from looking Timothy in the face.

Once released he ran after her but was quickly restrained "KHARMA!" He cried out.

"Get your fucking hands off me!!"

"KHARMA!!"

Kharma turned her head towards Timothy's direction with her lips she told him "No!" he stopped in his tracks as he read her lips

"It's okay I love you," the words mimicked off her lips.

"I love you too," he said back as he watched the love of his life being taken to jail.

"Kristie why would you do some shit like that I thought you and Kharma talked that shit out!"

Timothy was red in the face his grip on Kristie was firm "Get off!"

"This is none of your damn business Timothy and as far as I am concern she rot in the smallest jail cell they have for what she has done to my sister!"

"Your sister and just in the hell is that?!"

"Long story, I'm outta here" Kristie got into her car and drove off.

Melita had stayed upstairs until the coast was clear emerged with her belongings and some of Ka'Son's.

"Timothy can you take us to the bus station? I have told Kharma's father about everything that is happening, he is an attorney he will fix this but for right now Kharma asked me to keep Ka'Son safe and I will be taking him back home to Aurora with me."

Timothy looked as if he would break down at any moment's time "Mrs. Gomez why wouldn't she tell me something anything would have been better than the feeling that I have right now at this very moment!"

Melita sat down beside Timothy on the sofa the dog he had just gotten her was also positioned at his ankle "Son look at me, Kharma is not one to seek help nor does she wish for sympathy; when that mayor broke her heart she ran instead of seeking out her family for guidance."

"Feels like a thousand knives hitting me all at once. I should've protected her. Damn it Mrs. Gomez why or how could I not see that things were this serious with her past?!!"

"That's because love is stronger than any lie."

Melita felt sorry for Timothy, he had grown to love her daughter and her grandson unconditionally.

Timothy pulled himself together and grabbed his keys off the key holder on the wall beside the front door. He scooped up Evita and brought her to the bus station as well to see Melita and baby Ka'Son off.

"It was an honor meeting and getting to know you Dr. Timothy Stevens, I hope to see you again soon." Melita hugged her new found son in-law as he kissed Ka'Son goodbye as well.

Melita promised that he could come and visit anytime he would like.

Timothy watched as the bus carrying a baby boy he had taken under his wings drive off; he had no clue if he would in fact ever see little

Ka'Son again.

CHAPTER 13
(Black Balled)

Sebastian and Alonzo were watching the news when a familiar
face flashed across the screen.

News Report

*"Kharma Gomez, the suspect sought in the murder of Mayor
Adam D. Harris was captured and taken into custody today
at her home in Franklin, TN."*

*Gomez seemed to have been living with a friend at the time of
her apprehension. She will be transported back to Aurora
where she will undergo trial. There are no more updates on
this situation at this time."*

"Dad, what the hell is this for real?!"

"Lonzo, watch your mouth" Sebastian instructed him in a very
calming voice

"I'm sure your mother is right there with her and she
is going to get all this taken care of , we have one of the best
damn attorneys in town on our side right now."

"Well where is he who is?"

"Son your father is one of the best got damn lawyers West
Virginia has ever had, or did you forget that little issue?"

"That's all good dad but sitting here chatting about it isn't going to help Kharma. I mean we should be right there with her protecting her. Dad you know she is not built for things like this!"

Sebastian made some phone calls to see if he could get a bail and as it stands she is now the only suspect; Lana Harris has been ruled out as the number two suspect in the case.

Alonzo paced back and forth trying to gather his thoughts. Kharma was his big sister she has always looked after him. This time around it seems as if he would be the one protecting her.

"Well, well, look who it is front and center face just all over the TV." Lana Harris whispered to herself while catching the special update concerning her husband's murder.

"Lana who is that?"

"Who mom?"

Sidney points to the television set, "That young woman there in handcuffs and why is she being arrested for Adam's murder?"

"Mom really if she is being arrested don't you at least think that she

was the one to have shot my husband in cold blood?"

"She looks like a nice young lady"

"Yes so nice that she was lusting after and having an affair with my husband!"

"That does not make her a murder Lana. Maybe the sheriff made a mistake." Lana looked her mother who felt sympathy for Kharma, "Mother are you my mom or hers?"

"Oh stop Lana I was just trying to give the child the benefit of the doubt."

"See mama we gone all be dead with you giving people the benefits of the doubt."

Sidney laughed at her very comical daughter. Lana sat in the view of the television set for a while, she wasn't the sympathetic type at all when it came to pay back she was the queen of it; the way she saw it Kharma was getting everything she deserved for breaking up her home. She hadn't come to terms; that her marriage to the unfaithful mayor was already borderline broken.

Kharma was not afraid of what the people of Aurora thought, her silence was key. What's understood needs no explanations? She herself knew the truth and she would hold on to it regardless of what anyone thought of or had to say concerning her life.

The sheriff's department was swarming with cameras and news reporters and people wanting to know and see the face of the killer who took the life of their well-loved mayor. You would think that this would cause Kharma to buckle under pressure.

To avoid the crowd Kharma was taken around to the back of the county jail house.

"Kharma, now I want you to just speak openly and free when the investigator ask any questions. The more honest you are with us the better we can help you in all of this okay?"

Kharma gestured that she understood what Sheriff Simmons was telling her.

"Kharma sweetie can I get you anything to eat or maybe to drink?"

"Yes, can I have a bottle of water my throat is kinda dry."

Deputy Batemon catered to her every need. It was usual to see someone he had known since she was just a child in handcuffs and accused of murder.

Investigator Rowland came into the booking office and escorted Kharma to the interrogation room along with another official who would be recording her confession if he would lucky enough to get one out of her.

The Interrogation

"Kharma, this is Officer Joey and I am Investigator Rowland do you realize and understand why you are here?"

"I sure do Investigator Rowland I am not a child there is no need to sugar coat anything for me; if you have a question you should ask it."

Kharma was beyond the toying around, if they wanted to know if she had killed Adam then why not just come on out and say it. "You want to know how I knew Mayor Harris?" "I worked for him in his office; I started as an intern and ended up his full time personal assistant as well as the mother of his love child.

"Did I kill him? I was there yes. Did I pull the trigger on that gun, well I don't know Investigator Rowland you tell me?" Investigator Rowland took a deep breath and placed the gun on the table "You mean this gun, the same gun that has your fingerprints on it?!"

Kharma sat for a moment and stared at the weapon used to murder the father of her son Ka'Son. What was she to say now? Evidence never lie, especially if it's concrete.

Just as Kharma began to speak the door to the interrogation room swung opened.

"Kharma do not say another word!"

Sebastian Gomez ordered his daughter.

"What the hell is this Peter; you know damn well that she should have her attorney presence before she answers any questions or give any kind of confession!"

"This is protocol you know that Sebastian now can I finish my job?"

"GOT DAMN IT PETER YOU DO AND I WILL SUE YOUR ASS!"

Peter Rowland backed out of the room "You have 10 mins tops, either way she will be jailed until her court date."

"Daddy what are you doing here?"

"You didn't think I'd allow you to go through this alone?"

Sebastian Gomez hugged his timid daughter.

"Daddy, I cannot allow you to be my attorney."

"I don't understand sweetheart, why not?!"

Kharma hung her head "Daddy come on would it be fair to have my father knowing that you will represent me not out of ethics, but because I am your daughter and you will see me as such and not some criminal on trial?"

"Makes sense so tell me who'd you have in mind?"

"Attorney Harper."

Sebastian cleared his throat "Harper?!"

"Yes daddy, trust me on this okay?"

Sebastian Gomez kissed his daughter on her forehead, "you got it princess I'll get him down here right away in the meantime you tell those bastards nothing!"

"Okay." Kharma promised her father.

"Peter, she is not talking until Harper gets here so stay away from her."

Investigator Rowland smiled "Sure thing Sebastian like I said before we have a solved case in the making so it doesn't matter to me!"

Sebastian's nerves were starting become worked up "We will see about that Peter!"

Sebastian waved goodbye to his daughter and got on his job as her father and supporter he went out to his car and called up Harper

"Attorney Harper here."

"Harper what's up man it's Sebastian, is this a bad time?"

"Oh no I was just doing some last minute briefing; I have a huge case coming up."

"Right the Johnson's case. Well listen man you know they took Kharma into custody today, right?"

"I caught that, so are you going to represent her?"

"That's why I called you she asked for you to represent her."

Harper paused "I don't understand why?"

"Believe me I was in shock as well, but will you be able to do this or not? I mean this would mean a lot to me and Melita man."

"Look Sebastian no need to explain you know I got you, I'm on my way just stay with her until I make it there; make sure she says nothing."

"Appreciate it man see you there."

Harper collected his briefcase and headed out the door; just as he was about to pull out his garage he receives a phone call from the last person he wanted to hear from at that moment and point of time.

"Lana what is it I am in a hurry and I cannot do this right now."

"It's like that where you off to in such a hurry, did you see the news they caught Kharma Gomez?"

"No, actually Sebastian just told me that is where I am heading Kharma asked me to represent her and I agreed."

Lana grew silent *"You agreed to do what?!"*

"Really Harper?!"

"Listen first of all bring that tone down woman this is my job now I don't give a damn about your personal feelings concerning the Gomez's I have a client to get to I'll talk to you later."

Lana Harris for some reasons unknown to Harper frowned on his

choice to help Kharma Gomez on this case.

"Mother, come here, you and father for a second!"

Sidney and Albert Malone raced to the side of their daughter

"Lana what's wrong are you okay child?!"

"Yes listen you and dad watch the children while I run into town?"

"Lana for what now, you haven't been around these children since you buried Adam!"

"Mother this is not up for a debate now this is important."

Albert gave his wife a look showing his disapproval. "Sure Lana but you won't be making this a habit that little girl in there and your son needs you."

"Understood Dad, thank you I will be right back," she kissed them both and quickly left out the door.

Sidney walked over to Aimee and little AJ who had positioned themselves in front of the television.

"Grandma, does mommy hate us?" Litte AJ asked.

"No sweetheart why would you even ask that?"

"Well, she is never home, she always have somewhere to go."

"Daddy never ran away from us." Sidney tried to calm her tearful grandson.

"Stupid!"

"Aimee Harris!"

"He's stupid, mother hated daddy and now she hates us!" Aimee ran off into her room to be alone. Little AJ held on to Grandma Sidney as Grandpa Albert fixed up some lunch for them.

CHAPTER 14
(The Plan)

"Lonzo, where is your father?"

"Mom where are you? Kharma is about to be jailed, dad is with her."

"Listen, I need you to go over to Jonathan's house and ask him if he would come and pick me and the baby from the bus station."

"Wait you have Kharma's baby with you?"

"Yes, now do as I asked!"

"Geesh no need to yell I'm on it."

Alonzo rushed over to Jonathan's house just as he was about to head into town himself.

"Yo wait up man I need a favor could you take me to pick up my mother and my nephew from the bus station in town?"

"Nephew, you mean Kharma's baby is here in Aurora. Where the hell is Kharma bro?"

"Man haven't you been watching the news they arrested her for the murder of Adam."

"Bro seriously do not shit me right now your sister be a little on the crazy side but she is not a freaking murder!"

"Yeah I'm still stuck on the crazy part."

"Look let's just go get my mother."

Within ten minutes they were pulling into the bus terminal and inside waiting were Melita and baby Ka'Son.

"Mom, are you ready, are we going home to the jail house?"

"We are going to be by your sister's side Lonzo. Here take Ka'Son."

Alonzo was in aww over this chubby baby he had held. He was all too happy and very much like Kharma in many ways already. "Hey lil man I'm Lonzo;

Jonathan observed, "Okay dude that's just weird and do not ever sound like that around me again."

"Hello Mrs. Gomez nice of you to think of me on this day of intensity."

"Jonathan just drive this means nothing, I still think you are a bad seed."

Jonathan took that as a compliment "Thanks sugar."

"Investigator Rowland where is my client?"

"Well if it isn't old Harper, damn man long time no see, I thought you would still be in upstate Washington somewhere."

"You thought wrong, I'm still here and as of now the appointed attorney for Kharma Gomez."

"So Sebastian called in reinforcements, Nice!"

"Actually his daughter requested me."

The slick ass smile Peter Rowlands had on his face vanished as Harper made his way into the interrogation room where he found a very still Kharma waiting on his arrival patiently.

"Kharma, I got here as fast I could are you okay. How they been treating you so far?"

"I'm fine Mr... Harper now tell me what can you do to help me?"

"Well first thing's first just how much have you already told the other officials out there, cause they can and will use that against you."

"I told the truth, that I was there yes, but I will not speak on anything either or."

"Okay Kharma to better help you I will need you to help me and tell me truth."

Kharma finally gave in and told the truth that everyone was searching for; at the end of the day she would be escorted down to a holding cell until her awaited court date.

Melita would not accept this, not her child, not her daughter, she couldn't have committed this act of rage and jealousy; she loved Adam too much to harm one hair on his head.

"NO, NO, WHERE ARE YOU TAKING OUR DAUGHTER?!"

"SEBASTIAN DO SOMETHING PLEASE, STOP THEM THEY'RE TAKING HER AWAY!!"

"Melita! Compose yourself she gave a full confession there is nothing more I can do now!"

"God! My baby please god no!" Melita dropped to her knees as her husband kneeled beside her and held her in his arms, trying to console her crying. Alonzo held on tightly to Ka'Son as he himself tried not to break down.

"For what's it worth Sebastian, I will not stop until she is free you can bet on that. I'll be setting up a meeting with the assigned judge in the next few days."

"Hey man I know you will do all you can and more."

Sebastian shook hands with Harper. On their way out the doors of the jailhouse Lana Harris eagerly pushed past them.

"Lana what are you doing here?!"

"I do think that it's known of your damn business Sebastian."

"Listen to me you evil bitch IF I find that you had anything to do with this in any way I will make sure you pay for it understand me?!"

Sebastian had no care in the world now that his daughter was locked away like some hardened criminal.

"Smart move to threaten me in a room full of law officers very smooth."

Lana turned and proceeded to walk toward the direction of the holding cells.

"Officer, can me and Ms. Gomez here have some girl time?"

"Sure thing ma'am."

"Thank you."

Lana watched as the guard left them alone, but was standing not too far away.

Once she was sure that they were alone she began her conversation with the woman accused of killing her husband.

"How they treating you in here girl, you okay you need anything?"

"Yeah, some dick, can you bring that to me on a golden platter?" Kharma insisted.

Lana unsure asked Kharma "Did you stick to the story?"

"Of course I did. Do you realize how hard it is to lie to my family?"

"I can imagine, I have to keep a straight face at all times when pretending not to like your ass," Lana laughed.

This was the perfect plan since day one when it was hatched by the two scorned ladies.

Memory Lane

The night that Kharma signed that contract with Adam the rain poured down more than usually. Kharma couldn't believe that man she had given herself to had done this to her, to them, to their unborn child. As she walked home with all her hopes and dreams of being with the man of her dreams going down the drain, just as she had gotten closer to her home, she heard the sound of a car horn honking at her vigorously trying to obtain her attention.

"Kharma girl don't act like you don't see me blowing at you!"

The familiar voice called out to a distraught Kharma

She turned around and began to walk slowly to the car "Are you going to get in or are you going to stand in the rain all night shit really don't make me no difference?"

Kharma recognized the voice it was Lana Harris and she had no idea what the hell this bitch wanted with her.

"Damn, you act like somebody out to get you; relax boo I have a proposal I think you might like."

"Lana don't humor me okay, as far as I am concern you and that fake ass kindness act can go straight to hell!"

"How far along are you?"

"Excuse me?"

"You heard me how far along pregnant with my husbands' child Kharma?"

"Does it matter to you, he doesn't want it nor me, so why the fuck are you even here Lana?!"

"Hold on boo you can bring that base out ya voice mamas because this ain't that at all. I asked your irrelevant ass a simple question, of course he don't want it; what you thought he was going to leave his home and come be with you and that bastard baby you are carrying?!"

"What bitch?"

"Look Kharma you put yourself in this position you knew he was married but know this I am far from being dumb. I knew my husband was fucking you but see the only reason why I put up with it is because I have put up with way too much to even think about leaving and allowing a side chick to take my throne."

"So what do you want with me?"

"I want you to help me break his trifling ass down, take everything he has, and get what is due to me. This would be your perfect chance to get back at him for abandoning you?

"Wait, what is in this for me?"

"I'll make sure you and your baby will be well taken care of. As well as be an important factor in my children's lives as well."

"Listen all you have to do is take the fall for killing him; when it's done and you go to court I will be right there to set the records straight."

"Really, are you outta your fucking mind Lana? I will not agree to this shit!"

"Oh come on girl I got you boo; look he hurt both of us now are you in or out?!"

"Either way I win boo."

Kharma reflected for a moment and finally agreed, that night Lana Harris had gained a new partner in crime. She would leave as planned and when she had the baby she would come back to carry out the perfect plan.

"Listen Kharma I gotta go make sure you tell them what they want to hear and without giving away the plan.

"I gotcha."

"Well I gotta go boo I need to go be with my babies things have been so crazy lately I haven't been for them like I should."

"Yea I understand that, I once made that mistake, but never again."

"I saw your brother out there holding on to a baby boy, is he Adam's?"

"Yes that's my baby Ka'Son."

"He's beautiful Kharma."

"Thanks."

"GUARD!"

Kharma waved at Lana as she had heard the door close and lock behind her.

"Harper?"

"Lana, I'm working."

"I wouldn't care if you were bailing your mother out of jail, Harper I need to speak with you and now!"

Harper came to the aide of Lana just to keep her from getting so loud with him and embarrassing him.

"Damn it Lana what the hell is it, what do you want with me?!"

Lana snatched away from his clutches "I want you off this case and now!"

"Last time I checked Lana dear, my mother and father were both in Jersey!"

Harper, looked at her with the most distasteful look ever from a man to a woman.

"I'll talk to you later about this!"

During the drive home Sebastian had turned the radio down. Melita was still in a state of shock and Lonzo was enjoying his nephew, making goo goo sounds at him and playing peek-a-boo.

"Sebastian this has to be a mistake they made her say those things Kharma would have never harmed anyone not even if she herself were being threatened."

"Sweetheart, Kharma is your daughter through and through you know as well as I do no one can make her say anything she don't want to."

Melita searched for a form of reassurance in what her husband was telling her. She knew that it would be the state versus Kharma and she wouldn't stand a chance no matter how good of an attorney they hire for her.

Pulling up to their home Melita noticed a familiar face and was ever so glad to know that this person had come to support Kharma.

"Mom there is a strange man standing on our porch," Alonzo whispered into his mother's ear.

"Mom, are you cheating on dad?"

Melita smacked her teeth at her son's not so entertaining humor of a question.

"NO boy that is Dr. Timothy Stevens, he's here for Kharma he loves her."

"Poor guy."

"Lonzo that is enough, no more jokes for the rest of the day."

"Sorry dad just trying to lighten things up a little."

"Melita Gomez! I swear I am happy to you see again." Timothy greeted his new found mother in law with a hug.

Sebastian clears his throat "Oh, honey this is Dr. Stevens he took great care of our daughter and our grandson little Ka'Son there."

"Nice to meet you doctor, I am sure you realize that Kharma is jailed at the holding facility downtown."

"Yes sir, in fact that's my next stop. I just had to make sure that Melita and Ka'Son got here safely."

"How on earth did you get here so fast?"

"Well my family owns this small air strip and private jet so I got my pilot to get me here as fast as he could."

Sebastian seemed impressed at this man's strong will to come
to the side of his only daughter.
"And you must be Alonzo, Your sister talked about you all the
time in Franklin."
Timothy bragged while shaking Alonzo's hand.
"Well I don't wanna keep you folks I am heading over to the
hotel to check in and relax, I understand I won't be able to see
Kharma until tomorrow morning."
"Yea visiting hours are over until then, but hey man you can
stay here if you want you can sleep in Kharma's room I know
she would love that."
"I appreciate that Mr. Gomez."
"Ahh please just call me Sebastian. Mr. makes me sound old.
Ha ha. I'm still new to the grandfather phase,"
Sebastian Gomez chuckled.
"Hey Lonzo need some help with that cargo there?"
Alonzo handed Ka'Son over to Timothy who was reaching for
him.
"Well your bags are lighter than my little nephew over there."
They all laughed while entering the house.

CHAPTER 15

(The Living Dead)

That night in Aurora Jonathan Short had been at a friend's house partying and had just a few drinks. In the town of Aurora drinking and driving was the number one reasons young people ended up behind bars especially college kids who love to binge drink.

His usual route home involves him driving pass the National Stone graveyard at night. On this particular night Jonathan learned why it's not good to drink and drive.

Stopping to take a piss he noticed that he was the only one out there on the road and it was dark and creepy. Crackling noises could be heard in the distance and barking dogs nearby.

One loud sound of someone or something walking on the frostbitten grass in the graveyard caught Jonathan's attention.

"Who's there?!"

"Come on you guys, I'm not at all the least bit afraid so you might as well show yourselves!"

Jonathan zipped his pants quickly and got back into his car. Upon turning his ignition he caught sight of what appeared to be a ghostly woman dressed in all black holding a single white rose in her hands just standing in the shadows watching him as he drove off. The strange woman watched him as he passed her. Once out of view he stopped to glance into his rear view mirror and see what had he just witnessed but to no avail the strange woman in all black was nowhere to be seen.

With the site of the woman a long lost memory already, Jonathan decided it was time for him to stop drinking. Later that night Lana Harris decided it was only right to go to the grave site of her husband and reflect on some things. The wind was calm that day the clouds seem to play hide and seek with the sun. Lana had worn the traditional black dress a dress should've have worn during her husband's funeral. She was not alone she had brought Aimee and little AJ along with her as well. The children had asked their mother to come along with her to visit their father. This was not what Lana needed at this moment; when she and her children stepped foot into the graveyard she noticed someone leaving Adam's grave site

"HEY, WHAT ARE YOU DOING AT MY HUSBAND'S GRAVE?!" She scolded this person who ignored her and continued to walk away.

"Mommy who was that at daddy's grave?" Little AJ asked
"You know what sweetie I have no idea." Lana watched as the person walked out plain site.

She held her children close as they approached Adam's grave. Aimee was hesitant but finally gave in and welcomed her mother's guidance.

"Daddy I wish you were here, things are so different now that you have gone away. Grandpa Albert has been teaching AJ how to throw and pitch a fastball. Grandma helps with the cleaning around the house and well mommy is hardly at home I guess she has better things to do!" Aimee cried.

"Dad, it's AJ I brought you my favorite baseball. I want you to teach baby Jesus how to pitch just as you did with me." Little AJ placed the baseball in front of his father's headstone. They stood there in silence for a while before leaving and going home.

While driving home Lana tried to wrap her mind around the unknown person at Adam's grave. She could've sworn that everyone they both knew attended his memorial services.

"Mom, can we go for some ice cream?"

"Yeah ice cream!" Little AJ cosigned with Aimee.

"Ice cream huh welllll."

181

"Pleaseeeee!" the two children sung together.

"Okay you brats' two scoops and one topping each deal?"

"Deal mommy."

The *"Every Color of the Rainbow"* ice cream shop was just a few blocks from the office that once served as the pillar of every citizen's heard voice in Aurora.

"Aimee what would you like?"

Aimee searched the different flavors and toppings there were so many to choose from.

"I want vanilla and raspberry sherbet with a cherry on top," Little AJ told the ice cream man.

"Coming Right up little man."

"And what can I get for you little lady?"

"Mmmmmm I'll have vanilla and orange sherbet it was my father's favorite."

"You got it," the ice cream man replied with a smile.

"Anything for you ma'am?" He asked Lana.

"No not today," she smiled.

"Okay we are going to eat this here because y'all are not spilling ice cream all over my car I just had it shampooed."

Lana and the kids found a booth to sit and enjoy.

Lana was on her phone updating her Facebook status when she overheard some giggles and whispers over at the next table. She paid it no mind until she overheard one of the heffas mention, "Yea that's wifey."

"Aimee watch your brother." She got up and walked over to where these rough around the edges looking females were sitting.

"Now what were you ladies addressing before I walked over here?"

The boldest of them seemed more of a suburban type chick. She had long black hair with a caramel skin complexion. She wore leggings and UGG boots with a blouse that said Spoiled on the front.

"It sure wasn't you, so can you leave our table?"

"No, first of all you sent for me boo be clear on that. Secondly yes I am wifey and you are?" Lana challenged the girl.

"Shannon tell her who you are," one of her friends instigated.

"I knew your hubby, who do you think bought these boots I'm sporting?"

Lana was unbothered, "No sweetie your coochie paid for those boots. See I'm a Boss, I can sit on my ass seven days a week and still manage to sport a bad ass ride. You on the other hand

can't even afford to treat your girls here out to some real
dessert, and to top it off y'all sharing a sundae."
The girl's facial expression grew priceless as her friends waited
for her to clap back.
"Oh and by the way Shannon I must admit my old boots can
fit you, Adam was right we do wear the same size. You ladies
enjoy. On second thought here take that and treat your clique
or whatever to a nice phat Burger King meal," Lana insulted as
she tossed a $20 dollar bill on the table.
"99 cents menu boo" Lana instructed as she turned and
walked away leaving Shannon and her girls in shock.
"Shit bitch fuck this ice cream, let's go to Burger king!"
"Shut up Monica!"
Shannon feeling shitty and embarrassed demanded to her
friend.
"Mom are those girls' friends of Daddy's?" Aimee asked
"Not at all baby girl. Are you'll ready to get home?"
"Yeah" both the children replied.
"KRISTIE!" Miss Carlene what have you done child.
"What do you mean grandmother?"
"Do not play dumb with me, WHAT DID YOU DO?!"
"Look Grandmother, Kharma was not who you thought she

was, as far as I'm concerned it did us both a favor!"

Miss Carlene walks up to Kristie and slaps the hell out of her.

Smack!

Kristie stood in shock, as her grandmother had never raised her hands at her like that before.

"You better pray Ka'Son doesn't have to grow up without a mother or you will end up without a home!"

Kristie stood in the middle of the room that stood as room and board for baby Ka'Son and Kharma. She walked over Ka'Son's crib picked up a blanket Kharma had left behind and smelled it still smelled of him and his baby lotion.

Miss Carlene had grown to unconditionally love Kharma and Ka'Son and Kristie knew this but bitterly did the unthinkable by turning her into the cops.

Kristie went to comfort her grandmother who wept as if she had just lost her very own child.

"Grandmother?"

"Leave me alone Kristie, girl I can't look at you right now!"

"I'm sorry, if it means anything."

"I am not the one you should be apologizing to; how on earth you can sleep at night knowing you took that little boy's mother away from him!"

By this time Miss Carlene was in tears over this unforgivable thing her granddaughter had done. Kristie knew that no matter what she had done or said it wouldn't stop her grandmother's heart from aching.

"Gomez you have a visitor; keep it short and sweet lover boy." Sheriff Simmons voice alerted Kharma of a well awaited guest.

"Rise and shine beauty!"

"Timothy!"

"God baby what are you doing here, shouldn't you be at the clinic?"

"Trust me I am where I need to be right here, right now."

"Is that right Dr. Stevens?" Kharma seductively replied

"Dido"

Kharma laughed at how cute and charming Timothy was being.

"I went by your mother's house I had the honor of meeting your father and brother."

"Oh no not Alonzo, was he being a pest?"

"No actually we bonded quite well. Your parents even insisted that I sleep in you room while I am here in town."

"Baby why didn't tell me everything I could've helped out in some sort of way."

Kharma shook her head in doubt, "Timothy baby I doubt very much you could help my situation because it's much more complex than that."
"I know people who know even bigger people than Kharma, so never doubt me."
She signaled to kiss him through the iron bars that held stood between her and her man.
"I love you Dr. Stevens"
"I love you too Ms. Gomez"
"Times up lover man!" The guard called out as he opened the door to the visiting area leading Timothy out and leaving Kharma in tears.
Kharma had been so strong in all this long time but the moment she laid eyes on Timothy Stevens she became like a child who needed to be held and her emotions began to get the best of her. She wished she hadn't been so blinded, she wish she hadn't fallen for Adam Harris, and she wished that she could hold her baby once more.

CHAPTER 16
(Only the Strong Survive)

It had been a long week for everyone. Melita Gomez was keeping busy by caring for Ka'Son. Sebastian took on small court cases while Alonzo continued to attend school and Dr. Stevens took on a small job as the town's head doctor. Life in the mayor's mansion changed as well. Lana had become more and more hands on with Aimee, there were no more outbursts from her about her father.

Sidney and Albert Malone had both moved into the mansion just until the entire ordeal was over. Lana and Attorney Harper grew closer by the day. Some days they'd meet up in his office just catch a quickie.

"Mr. Harper you have a client."

"Send them in Margaret," he radioed to his assistant.

"Mr. Harper, I was wondering if you would take a look at my case for me I've been all over but no one seems to be in a position to help me and I was told that you were the best in town." It was Lana Harris dressed for role playing.

"Well you know ma'am my prices are a little steep can you afford them?"

Lana opened the leather trench coat she had worn revealing nothing but her birthday suit and some "fuckem shoes."

"Now let's see where I put that money, I know I put it here somewhere."

"Here allow me to help you with that."

Harper slowly walked over to Lana and searched every inch of her body with his tongue; he knew that with Lana being a boss she wouldn't mind a little roughness. Harper instructed her to close her mouth.

He snatched her coat from her nude body and demanded her to bend over. "Hands on the desk, ass up, and don't say shit!" Harper demanded.

He pulled her hair as he fucked her doggy style on his office desk. Lana, who knew he did not want to be heard, folded her lips and let out silent cries.

"This is what you want right?!"

"I-I- yes Harper Damn!" The two went at it like two wild animals in the deep Amazon jungle.

Stroke after stroke Lana's body began to quake and then a line of juices began to frantically stream down her thighs.

He stares at her "Is that what that Rican pussy of yours wanted?"

Lana licked her lips and passionately kissed his lips. She said nothing, she flashed a smile and left the office of Attorney Harper. Once in the privacy of her own car she pulled a recorder from the pocket of the coat she had been wearing and played back the entire ordeal. The biggest smile took over her face "Stupid motherfucker, I realize I'd rather keep the trash and throw you out." It had been a set up. Lana trusted no man and she made sure she would always have the upper hand on them. One wrong move and she would send this recording to the chairmen of the law firm and show them just how Harper's clients pay for his representation.

"Mr... Harper, are you okay in here I heard a lot of bumping and banging in here!"

Harper blushed as he knew what his temp was hearing; it was the sound of him beating that pussy up on Lana from the back.

"Melita, I wanted to send my dearest apologies to you and your family. I know this must be a very difficult time for you all."

"Thanks father Joseph, you know I have cried and cried and no matter how much I pray, I wake up every morning and nothing seems to have gotten better; Kharma is still in that god awful place!"

"You must not shy away from your faith Melita he hears and sees all, you will get through this."

"Oh save me the preaching FATHER if there is a God then why is my only daughter sitting in JAIL!"

Melita stormed out the church she had come to for some quiet time but even that place seemed too noisy.

No matter how strong she fooled herself into being Melita was no match for the hurt and pain she felt when it came to her children. She decided to take a ride around the town just to clear her head and be alone. She had left Ka'Son with Timothy until she returned.

Timothy decided to take Ka'Son to see his mother hoping that would maybe brighten up her day.

"Wait a minute now son you can't take any kids into the holding area."

"Come on Sheriff, Kharma hasn't seen her son since you brought her in, at least do it for the child," Timothy asked of the Sheriff

"Alright make it quick, keep it simple." The sheriff signaled for the guard to let Timothy and Ka'Son in to see Kharma.

"Surprise look who came to see you Mama."

Kharma was more than surprised to see her baby boy in all smiles she had missed him so much and wanted no more than to hold him.

"Oh my god my baby Ka'Son, hi little man!" she reached out to him through the iron bars."

"Mommy!" Ka'Son uttered as her reached out to her as well.

Kharma smiled and cried all at once "He said it he called out to me Timothy did you hear him?!"

"Yes baby I did," he replied while placing a kiss on Kharma's lips.

"So, are there any updates on your case, has anyone else been in here to talk to you or anything?"

"No, I haven't seen anyone. Harper he's my attorney and I swear I have no communication with that man at all!"

Timothy thought to himself for a moment and came up with another idea "I have this attorney, he handles all my legal matters and has been for years now he is great."

"Can you call him up, if so how fast can he be up here?"

"I can tell him it's a state of emergency and he will be right out/"

"God! Thank you so much baby!"

"No problem, tell you what let's say our goodbyes and I'll get right on that for you."

Kharma kissed Timothy and Ka'Son goodbye and got on his job of helping his woman.

Kharma felt a sense of relief she knew that Timothy would not let her down. He would try his best to do what he should as her lover and as her friend. Harper who was too wrapped up in Lana had no clue that he was about to lose a client which would serve as a great feeling of amusement to Lana Harris.

Timothy's call

"Yea hey Mack it's Tim how you been doing?"

"You know me keeping busy, busy, busy, what's up?"

"Well it's my lady man she need your help she has an attorney but he ain't about shit when it comes to communication and I told her about you."

"So what you need me to represent her?"

"I swear it would be well appreciated"

"Man you know I got you, just give me her information and I'll get right on that for you."

"Good looking out, okay I'll email you her name and the cause of her needing an attorney; we're down in Aurora VA."

"Okay well I'll see you no later than 9am tomorrow morning."

"Thanks man!"

"No problem."

"Yes can I get a cup of green tea and a lemon on the side," Melita ordered at the diner where she had stopped to relax.

"Melita?"

"Yes?"

"Melita Gomez, It's me Jonathan's mother, Samantha, how are you holding up?"

"Oh hey hun I'm holding up okay, I suppose you heard the news about Kharma?"

"Yes it's just sad you know."

"No, I don't know, what's sad Samantha!"

"The fact that you had the nerve to call my son troublesome and you swore he was or would never be good enough to date your precious daughter. Well who's the troubled one now Melita?!"

Melita took a moment to keep calm and prayed with all her might that she wouldn't end up knocking this bitch out.

"Samantha, you're right but guess what nothing has changed I still feel she shouldn't date Jonathan at all!"

"I guess you are right I mean I don't need my son ending up dead as well like Mayor Adam!"

Without warning Melita attacked. "BITCH!" Melita had gotten so angry that before she knew it her fist was connecting with Samantha's face.

The people in the diner paused for a moment and went on about their business Samantha Short was known for being the messy bitch in town. She knew everyone's business she knew the what, when, why, and where. On a day like today she picked the wrong person to start shit with.

It has taken a lot for Melita Gomez to snap. She had enough she felt like she was going crazy. She decided to head back home where at least she could be at peace in the safety of her own home with her family. Once at home Melita found it odd that Alonzo's back pack was right there at the bottom of the stairs.

She looked her watch it was only 11:00 am so what was he doing home so early "Lonzo, are you up there?"

No one answered as she called out to her son once more, "Alonzo?!" Suddenly she hears this faint sound coming from her son's room. She walked slowly and quietly toward his bedroom door the sound grew and grew. Melita paused for a split second before twisting the doorknob "WHAT THE HELL?"

Alonzo had been home the entire time and having sex in his parent's house.

"Mom, I can explain!"

"Damn right you can, young lady I need for you to get the hell out of my house right now!"

The girl was ashamed and embarrassed "Please forgive Mrs. Gomez, please don't tell my father you saw me here."

Melita looked a little harder "Wait, Tabitha?"

"Does Deputy Batemon know that you skipped school today?!"

The girl hung her head "No ma'am."

"Well this time I will let this slide but next time I will take this up with your father!"

"Thank you Mrs. Gomez, I'm leaving now"

Melita watched as Tabitha headed down stairs and listened as her front door opened and closed shut.

Alonzo felt bad that his mother had to catch him in an awkward position at a time like this.

"Really Lonzo, in my home you bring her here to have sex with her in my home?!"

"Look Mom!"

"No you listen this is not the time to be babysitting you, you are old enough to know right from wrong!"

Melita firmly spoke to her son.

"Your sister would have never done anything like this!"

"So that's it, Mom I realize you are upset about Kharma but do not stand there and try to down size me!"

"That's not what I meant"

"Sure it is your precious daughter could do no wrong or harm in your eyes but I am always the screw up, NEWS FLASH MOM KHARMA MURDERED THE MAYOR OF OUR FREAKING TOWN!"

Smack!

Melita backed away as realizing that she had slapped her son out of pure anger

Alonzo looked at his mother with a glare, "Right, Feel better?"

He mouthed as he walked out of his bedroom leaving his mother in tears.

"Yo, Lonzo I need to speak with you bro!"

"Look Jonathan not now I have too much on my mind!"

"Nah, I said I need to speak with you right now!"

Alonzo finally gave in to Jonathan's request

he walked over to Jonathan who was also coming towards him

Pop!

Jonathan had punched Alonzo who wasn't expecting that at
all.

"THE HELL WAS THAT FOR BRO DAMMIT YOU PUNCHED
ME IN MY FUCKING EYE MAN!"

"NO SHIT, TELL YOUR BITCH OF A MOTHER TO KEEP
HER HANDS OFF OF MY MOM!" Jonathan got into his car
and dug off leaving tire marks in the middle of the road.

Alonzo was still kind of dazed from the punch as he staggered
to his feet Timothy who was just pulling in ran to his side to
help him on to his feet

"Whoa champ what happened to you?"

"Listen, thanks for the help but I rather not talk about it."

"Suit yourself, let's get you in the house and put some ice on
that."

"Mommy, there's some man here to see you,"

Aimee alerted her mother.

Lana who had been doing laundry wondered what man would
show up at her doorstep in the middle of the afternoon it

couldn't have been Harper he knows not to do that. "Who is it Aimee?"

"He says he knew Daddy."

"I'm coming."

Upon reaching the front door she noticed that it was Sebastian.

"What are you doing here Sebastian shouldn't you be at the firm?"

"I should but not until we have a talk first."

"Right now is not a good time I mean my parents are out and I have the children."

"Well can I come in?"

Lana thought about it for a second and finally allowed Sebastian to enter her home.

"Aimee, where are your manners girl speak."

"Hi Mr., I'm Aimee and this is AJ"

She introduced herself as well as her baby brother who had come to see the man at the door as well.

"Can I get you something to drink Sebastian?"

"Coffee, listen Lana is there somewhere privately we can talk?"

"In the study, after I pour this coffee."

They soon headed into the study as the kids watched television.

"Lana, why aren't the kids in school?"

"That's because I pulled them out of that awful school, they are to start their new school in the morning."

"So what is it Sebastian?"

"I wanted to start seeing Aimee; I think it's only right that she has her father there for her."

"Hold on, pause. Do you actually think that you can walk in here after Adam has raised her and play daddy?!" Lana laughed

"I wouldn't make it sound that blunt but yeah she's my daughter."

"NO, SHE'S MY DAUGHTER SEBASTIAN SHE WASN'T YOUR DAUGHTER WHEN YOU WENT BACK TO MELITA KNOWING SHE WAS FUCKING ADAM. YOU PROMISED TO BE THERE!!"

"Woman, what are you yelling for?!"

"You know what Sebastian get the fuck out!"'

"What why?!"

"You gotta go now!"

She pushed and shoved him until he was out the door.

CHAPTER 17
(Attorney Mack)

Attorney Mack had kept his promise and at exactly 9am he
was there in Aurora.

"Hi, may I help you sir?" The receptionist said

"Umm yes you may beautiful can you direct me to a Ms.
Kharma Gomez"

"Sure, now are you a lawyer or family member?"

"I'm her attorney."

"Okay well go right on back."

The guard brought Kharma into the visiting room.

"Kharma Gomez, Hi Timothy told me about you and I am sure
you have heard about me, I'm attorney Mack McCurry."

"Yes, I've heard about you nice to meet you."

Kharma shook his hand. She gave him this look of distrust as
he began to sort through all the details of her situation.

"Ms. Gomez I noticed that you were looking at me like I am no
more than a petty thief."

"You would have to forgive me but see I don't trust men easily
Attorney Mack."

"Well I assure you that I am true to my word and in my opinion after what you have been through I don't much blame you."

Kharma smiled "Are you trying to gain my trust sir?"

"Is it working?"

"Just a little now what can you do for me?"

"I can and will get you a fair trial no bullshitting around. Now there is a strong chance of you being found guilty, if this happens I can you a suspended sentence if you plea by reasons of insanity."

"Mr. Mack I am not crazy; since when does being heartbroken turn into someone being crazy? Okay I admit I may have threatened the lives of others, but they hurt me first and I wanted them to feel what I was feeling!"

"By all means, I mean an eye for an eye, I get it, but you have to look at it from the victim's loved ones point of views."

"Look it's not like I don't okay, I just want to know regardless will I at least see my son grow up and maybe have a family of his own one day?"

"Ms. Gomez I don't know what the Lord has planned for you, but I know that if you trust me in doing my job I will not sleep until you are justified."

Kharma liked his understanding and non-judgmental way of thinking. Just as Kharma began to sign Mr. Mack on as her lawyer, the doors to the visiting room swung open.

"There must some misunderstanding; you see this is my client!" It was Harper.

"I'm sorry and you are?"

"Attorney Harper, Kharma's personally appointed legal advisor,"

"Kharma, what the hell is going on here?!"

"Well Harper you acted as if I was relevant for just that one day and now you bust up in here and demand that you're my legal advisor?!"

Mack looked at Harper with competition in his eyes "Look Harper, lack of communication is the easiest way to lose a client!"

"It's HARPER, and I have no problems in that area Kharma knows that I am a busy man and she understands!"

Kharma looked over at Harper who sounded so sure of himself "What I understand is that you are so not professional and Attorney Mack here is willing to go beyond to help me, besides he ain't feeding me no bullshit!"

"What's going on in here?!" The sheriff checked in after hearing raised voices

"Nothing at all Sheriff, Mr. Harper here was just leaving." Harper adjusted his tie picked up his briefcase and walked calmly out of the room. This was his first time losing a client in this manner. Something in his gut was telling him that Lana Harris had her paws all over it and he will find out one way or the other. On his way to the car he made it his business to call her while it was still fresh on his mind.

Harper calls Lana

"You wicked bitch what have you done?!"

"Bitch, excuse me but your mother is nowhere around Harper!" Lana fired back.

"Oh I'm well aware of that, did you do it, was it you who sent Kharma some Tennessee Attorney?!"

Lana couldn't believe what she was being accused of "Puff really Harper what makes you think I would help her one bit?!!"

"Well somebody did it and damn it let me find out it really was your cold hearted ass!"

"Whatever, oh and next time say Ms. Bitch k sweetie talk to you later."

And the call ended on that note.

"Know what that bitch know something about this shit let me call Sebastian see what he knows."

Harper Phones Sebastian

"Sebastian Gomez here."

"Sebastian it's Harper so when was you going to tell me?!"

"Tell you what man?"

"Your daughter has a new attorney, did you know anything about this because you practically begged me to represent her!?"

"Pump your breaks okay I never begged you. You could've easily have said no and if she has someone else it was her doing not mine so do not blame or come at me!"

"Yeah, Right!" Harper ended the call on a sour note.

"I got something for all of you playing with my money oh I got something for you I swear just wait and see." Harper said talking to himself.

Knock

Knock

Harper turned to see a stranger knocking on his passenger side car window.

He rolled down the window to see if the person was lost and needed directions

"Hey, are you lost or something?"

"Yes, can you help me I'm looking for a great attorney around here, I have some information on the Gomez case and before I speak a word I would like legal protection."

"Well hop in this just may be your lucky day."

Harper unlocked his door and the stranger turned his client got in.

"HEY, anybody home?"

"In here Timothy, how was your day?"

"Mrs. Gomez, It was great two children came into the office and they were in awe over Ka'Son, I tell you the first thing I am going to do is have a daycare center built onto my clinic in Franklin the one in town is amazing."

Melita, placed a casserole in the oven before washing her hands and taking Ka'Son in her arms.

"Now let's get this little guy ready for a bath."

Ka'Son, enjoyed the baths his grandmother would give him truth be told he got more water on her than he did on his own self. This was something she wished her daughter was here to endure as his mother.

With the days to follow, Attorney Mack had done just what he had promised and within months of being arrested Kharma's first trial was to begin.

The judge of Kharma's trial was also from upstate. The defense would argue their case against Kharma Gomez and how she manipulated those around her including her friends, her family, and her peers.

"Kharma, are you ready, nervous?"

"Is it obvious?"

Kharma was a nervous wreck the day of her trial. She paced back and forth watching the clock "I -I can't do this Mack what if they just take one look at me and toss the book at me with no sympathy or no care in the world. I could be away from my son, my baby, for a very long time?"

"Just relax now I know the judge and he fair in everything he does, you will receive a fair shot here today and the days to come," Attorney Mack assured Kharma.

Meanwhile on the other side of Aurora Lana Harris was preparing herself as well as the kids for the trial. She decided she would appear to the courts as a grieving widow who was a total wreck without her husband. She had gained riches from his demise and was in a way happy that he was gone. The "son of a bitch deserved it" she smiled as she took portrait of their wedding off the wall and tossed it over the balcony.

"Lana Marie, do you really think it's good idea to take the children to the trial?"

"And why not Mom?"

Sidney stared at her daughter who was brushing her hair "Look at me!"

"DO not take these children through any more hell than they have already been through Lana; seeing their father in that casket was more than enough!!"

Lana rolled her eyes at her mother "Mom, listen it's fine they will be fine now could you go and help them get ready?"

Sidney saw that it was no use in trying to talk some sense into her daughter's head she was going to do exactly what she wanted when she wanted and no one would tell her otherwise.

"Grandmother, I don't want to go" Aimee confessed to her grandmother who had come to french braid her ponytail.

"Sweetie believe me your mother insists and I refuse to argue or fuss with her; she would only turn around and swear that I am calling her a bad parent."

"A man came over the other day while you and grandpa were out."

Sidney ceased in braiding Aimee's hair "what do you mean, was it the same man?"

"No, his voice was different, I couldn't understand what they were really saying but they were discussing me."

"I wonder who that could've been."

"I don't know but Mommy put him out, he made her angry I guess."

"Well child it doesn't take much to get on your mother's bad side and once that happens it's a wrap."

"There, all done now let me go and see how your brother is looking, lord knows your grandfather is not keen on matching."

"Albert, how are you coming along in there with AJ?"

"Well, what do you think?"

Albert had presented little AJ wearing knee length shorts with suspenders his socks were checkerboard and very long, stopping at his kneecaps.

"Oh my God, Albert what have you done to our grandson!?"

Sidney let out the loudest yelp followed by laughter.

"Lord baby come here let me see what I can do to help you here." Sidney changed little AJ's entire attire, when she was

finished he was now wearing a pair of polo jeans with a baby blue polo shirt and all white 23s to match "Now that's better!"
"I still say he should wear the suspenders?" Albert suggested as Sidney ignored him and his taste in kids fashion.
"Lana are you ready cause we are, Let's go and get this over with" Lana emerged from her bedroom looking as plain as she could wearing a silk red blouse and a pair of black slacks with no make-up and no jewelry, but she managed to keep her shoe game just right wearing red bottom's as always.
"Ready, let's go!"
Lana studied herself as the kids and her parents observed her not so fancy choice of attire to wear to court.
"What?!"
"Oh nothing" Sidney responded, they loaded up into two different cars and one trailed the other to the courthouse.
"Sebastian, honey are you ready to go?"
Melita called out to her husband who was getting dressed or so he claimed to have been after an hour or two of waiting on him to come down stairs she ran up to see what was keeping him.

"Why aren't you ready yet Sebastian, we have to go Kharma
needs us all to be there!"
Sebastian had stopped getting dressed and sat on the side of
the bed in him and Melita's bedroom.
"Melita I know this but I cannot maintain a professional
stance and listen to these people degrade our baby girl; as a
father my natural instinct would be to just protect her."
"Sebastian believe me I feel the same way, but still if you are
not there she will never forgive you and she will forever blame
me."
Sebastian found truth in what his wife was saying so he
proceeded to get dressed. Timothy,
Alonzo, and Ka'Son had long since left together.
The town was still that day; the diner wasn't as packed as it
had normally been. Some of the town's people decided to
attend the trial of Kharma Gomez. Some were there for
support of the Gomez's, others for their beloved mayor, and
the rest just to be nosey plain and simple. The news station
would be covering every aspect of the Gomez trial.

CHAPTER 18
(The People vs Kharma A. Gomez)

The trial started at 10am, the jury was there and seated promptly. The sheriff had already escorted Kharma into the courtroom to avoid the news cameras and her attorney Mack McCurry was seated beside her as well. She turned to her left and caught site of Timothy, her brother, and her baby boy sitting right behind her. She waved and blew kisses at them as she wondered to herself where could her parents be on the most important yet drastic day of her life.

"Where's mom and dad?" She mouthed silently to her brother who before he could answer pointed to the double doors leading to the courtroom as Melita and Sebastian came rushing through. Kharma was overwhelmed with happiness to see her parents as her mother walked up to her and placed a kiss upon her forehead.

"You made it!"

"We wouldn't allow you to fight this alone." Melita tucked Kharma's hair behind her ear for her "You are our baby girl." for once Kharma felt where her mother was coming from. No matter how old she gets or the kind of trouble she would get herself into they would always be there no questions asked.

Lana Harris along with her children and parents as well entered no sooner after Kharma parents had. She looked over at Kharma with the strangest look, although Kharma acted as if she didn't see or notice it at all.

Melita Gomez saw it and she didn't for one bit like it. "Why would she bring those babies to this trial?" She whispered to Sebastian.

"I have no idea maybe she wants the courts mercy."

"That's the saddest way to get it." Melita decided that she would as a mother ask Lana herself "Lana?"

"Oh hello Melita I did not see you sitting over there."

"Why in the hell would you even think about bringing those children to this court hearing?!"

Lana pointed towards Timothy "The same reasons you all chose to bring your grandson as well!"

"Ka'Son is only two years old, he doesn't understand any of this yet!"

"What's your point Melita?!"

"You know what, talking to you is pointless."

"Toddles" Lana laughed and waved as she watched Melita
walk off.

The Gomez trial begins

"All rise the honorable Judge Stanley Mathers Presiding."
The sounds of standing feet could be heard throughout the
courtroom. The court reporter began taking notes as
everyone started to be seated as instructed to do so when the
bailiff stated "You may all be seated."
The judge began reading the case files of the People vs
Kharma Gomez in the death of Mayor Adam D. Harris III.
Are both parties attorneys present at this time?"
"Yes your honor," the two answered at the same time.
Harper had gotten so upset about Kharma deciding not to
use him
that he went over to the Defendant side and he was
determined to place Kharma behind bars for a long time.
"Very well the Defense may argue their case." Judge Stanley
gave his approval
and Harper got up and began.
"Well I would like to start off saying that, I want you all to
take a good look at our accused Ms. Kharma Gomez. She's

beautiful, smart, and very conniving. Looks can be very deceiving and it just so happens that our late Mayor Adam D. Harris fell for her trap. During this trial I will not only prove to you that she is not the sweetheart that she plays out to be, but she without a doubt murdered Mayor Adam in cold blood leaving his children fatherless. Thank you".

Harper sat down adjusting his tie as he glance over at Attorney Mack and Kharma.

Mack began his defense for Kharma.

"This young lady may have made some bad decisions in life but who hasn't. Every single one of us including our law officials has done something that we regret every day of our lives; are they on trial here, are we sitting here degrading them?"

Mack looked at Harper and continued on "No, because the fact of the matter is Adam Harris seduced Kharma. He played with her, he lead her on, he used her for his own sexual pleasures, and when things got good with him and his wife again he dropped her; not only that he left her alone confused and pregnant. He then went as a far as to pay her to leave town. Now I ask you who the real criminal here is ladies and gentlemen?!"

"Both sides put up argument. Are there any witnesses to be called at this time?"

The judge asked both parties.

"Yes your honor, if it pleases the court I would like to call Kristie Armani to the stand."

Harper offered for the defense side.

"Raise your right hand and place your other hand over the bible, state your name please."

"Kristie Armani"

"Ms. Armani do you swear to tell the truth the whole truth and nothing but the truth so help you God?" The bailiff stated.

"Yes, I do."

"Ms. Armani tell us how do you know Ms. Gomez?" Harper questioned.

"Well she lived with me and my grandmother for two years off and on, she had her baby and right after that she abandoned him and we were left to care for him; That and the fact that my sister Kacey Armani would call me on a day to day basis giving me the gossip on Kharma and Adam. Kinda sad if you ask me. I mean why fall for a man who *could never truly love you the way he loved his wife or for that matter, my sister."*

Kharma looked on as someone who she once considered a sister turn on her.

"No further questions your honor."

"Your witness attorney McCurry," the judge spoke.

Mack clears his throat "Ms. Armani, you say that Kharma was obsessed is that right?"

"That's right and she was"

"Now what gave you that idea, did she talk about it daily what Adam had done to her?"

"No not exactly to be honest she never hardly said anything at all. She would normally talk to my grandmother."

"Ah ha and how did that make you feel Ms. Armani?"

"OBJECTION YOUR HONOR, Ms. Armani's feelings has nothing to do with her testimony here today!" Harper interrupted with an outburst.

"Objection Overruled, answer the question Ms. Armani" the judge replied.

"I-I resented her, I mean it was if she had come in and taken over my entire life and after all this time she had the nerve to show back up and play mommy after leaving that baby off

on my grandmother and she accepted Kharma back with opened arms!"

"So is it safe to say that you are a bit jealous of Kharma and your grandmother's relationship, is that why you're here today Ms. Armani?"

"Objection your honor this is irrelevant to the nature of this case and Ms. Armani here is not the one on trial!"

"Overruled!"

"That is not what this is Mr. McCurry and I will not sit here and allow you to make this out of some competition!" Kristie proceeded to defend her reasons of being there.

"YOU ARE UNDER OATH SO I ADVISE YOU TO HAVE A SEAT MS. ARMANI DO YOU OR DO YOU NOT HATE KHARMA GOMEZ FOR YOUR OWN PERSONAL REASONS. IS THIS NOT THE REASONS WHY YOU ARE HERE TODAY TO EVEN THE SCORE?!"

"YOU DAMN RIGHT THAT BITCH MURDERED MY SISTER KACEY ARMANI; YOU DAMN RIGHT SHE DESERVES TO FRY!"

Just than the court gasped in sudden shock and for a split second there was a sudden high volume of whispering going on.

The judge tried to calm the courtroom by banging his gavel
"Order I want order in this courtroom!!"
"Ms. Armani, do you have any proof of this murder?"
"No but I know she did it!"
"I have no further questions your honor."
"Ms. Armani, you may step down," the judge gave her
permission to do so.
"Okay it's lunch time let's take a break and be back in here at
1:30pm."

During the lunch break, Lana made it her business to
approach Kharma.

"Well, two for the price of one and I couldn't have thought of a
more perfect plan if I must say so myself"

"Lana, now is not the time what is it that you want?"

"Just wanna know why you fail to mention that someone else
knew about Kacey?"

"First of all I am not about to discuss that here with you okay,
now go away before people began to get suspicious.

Lana took to heart to what Kharma was telling her, they were
getting strange stares from some of the town's people. "Aight,
boo it's about that time get in there and give them all you got."

****

Part 2 of the Gomez Trial

"Your honor if it pleases the court I would like to enter item A as evidence."

Harper exhibited the gun used to shoot Adam.

"The people will allow it council," the judge signaled for him to bring forth the weapon.

Kharma glanced over at Lana who winked at her; no one still had no clue about their plan. Kharma didn't know just how long she would be able to continue on with this show. She sat and watched as a witness who claimed to have had insight on the situation make up lies and fabricate the truth.

"Council you may call your next witness to the stand please."

"I would like to call Jonathan Short to the stand your honor."

Harper had recruited Jonathan Short after the incident between Melita and his mother.

After being sworn in the questions began.

"Now, Mr. Short is it safe to say that Ms. Gomez is a dear and longtime friend of yours?"

"That's true, actually she and I dated on and off for a year and a half."

"THAT'S A DAMN LIE AND YOU KNOW IT JON!" Kharma was outraged

The judge hit his gavel down "Council control your client!"
He ordered Kharma's attorney.

Jonathan continued "Kharma, she was so clingy and so territorial. I mean whenever I was around her she was fine but if another woman came around that was it she would flip it was her way or the highway."

"And when you say clingy tell us in your own words what you had to endure when Ms. Gomez became too clingy."

"Well one night as I was sitting in my car she came out of nowhere on me I mean she had been hiding in my car the entire time and I had no idea. It sort of spooked me out."

"Thank You Mr. Short, no further questions your honor."

"You two had a relationship?" McCurry asked his client.

"No, he was and still is after me. I never gave him the time of day that's the truth!" Kharma whispered angrily to her attorney.

"Well now watch me work" McCurry fixed his tie and proceeded

"Mr. Short, you claim that you and my client had relationship for an over a year is that correct?"

"Yes sir."

"And she was as you put it clingy?"

"I couldn't get rid of her sir," Jonathan laughed.
"But the night she so called hid in your car Adam Harris asked you to follow her is that right?!"
"Well I-I may have talked to Adam that night."
"YOU ARE UNDER OATH NOW GIVE ME A STRAIGHT ANSWER MR. SHORT!" McCurry demanded the truth and was not going to stop until he had gotten just that.
"YES, I FOLLOWED HER FOR ADAM!"
"And why did you do it Mr. Short?"
"Because Adam asked me to, he paid me to do it."
"I see, no further questions your honor."
"Mr. Short you may step down."
"Court will resume tomorrow at said time of 9am, court is adjourned for today."
The judge had heard some crazy things in his days but this town and its secrets take the cake.

CHAPTER 19
(MISS CARLENE)

Kharma never figured in a million years that Jonathan would turn on her like that. Things were beginning to become clearer for Kharma Gomez now, all the friends she thought she had and thought she could trust had now become her sworn enemies. There was nothing worse than a salty ass man being pissed all because a woman refuse to fuck with his non relevant ass and Jonathan was that coward ass man.

Kristie was not as important, Kharma knew what to expect from her. That goes to show you the same ones you refer to as a sister would turn right around and stab you in the back. Kristie had made her seem like an unfit mother, some love crazed person who cared more about a no good ass man than her own child, which was so very far from the truth.

Kharma was taken back to her holding cell at the jailhouse.

"Deputy Batemon, can I ask you a question?"

"Sure Kharma"

"Do you think that God forgives all sins even those that were done without care?"

"I believe that we are all humans and with that being said it's in our nature to make mistakes." Deputy Batemon knew what Kharma meant he just wasn't into selling her bullshit story. Pulling into the parking lot of the jailhouse, Kharma noticed very familiar vehicle.

Walking into the jailhouse she also noticed a very familiar face "Miss Carlene!"? Kharma was overwhelmed with joy. She knew with her being there it would make things a whole lot easier on her.

"I'm glad to see you too Kharma, how is it going for you. I saw Kristie testify against you I tried to stop her but that child has a mind of her own." Miss Carlene tried to make excuses for her granddaughter.

"No, Miss Carlene it's really alright, Kristie is just unhappy with herself and her life as well."

Miss Carlene smiled at the sweet person Kharma was or had become. This was not the same girl that had walked through her door in Franklin two years ago. She was at peace and that was key. She was happy to be a mother and she held no grudge against no one.

"Well, I am happy to see you doing well Kharma, you know you are just like my own and I love you."

"I love you too Miss Carlene!" Miss Carlene hugged her and went on her way. She had only came in town to see Kharma and Ka'Son which she saw him and played with him after court had turned out for the day.

Kharma could see the look on Miss Carlene's face it was if she were waiting and searching for some sort of answer from her. She wanted so much to tell her the truth and to tell everyone that has ever asked her since this thing had begun.

"Bitch you are crazy if you think that I'm just going to let you walk up in here and give me orders!" Lana looked at the ratchetness of Shannon the girl she had to check at the ice cream store that day.

"Boo, it's not what you are going to let me do it's what I will do, I don't want your ass nowhere near this community center or the office. There are more deserving women and children who need the assistance and you are not one of them!"

The girl had come to fill out an application for the housing assistance program that Adam Harris had started before he died. This chick was from the suburbs and Lana Harris was no fool at all she knew this bitch was being sarcastic as hell but she had the right one though.

Miss Carlene didn't leave right away. She decided to go take a look around the town of Aurora. There were a lot good thrift stores and flower shops there as well. She went into one called *Crimson Rose*. The shop was filled with all different types of species of roses. These flowers were not only grown in America but also in exotic places as well. There were all shades of the rainbow and more. She purchased some seeds to grow her garden of exotic roses.

Melita sat in silence on her front porch and snared at the fact that Jonathan Short made her daughter look like some lunatic. The rest of the day was quiet yet long. The sun had begun to set.

"Sweetheart, are you coming inside, or are you going to sit out here all evening?"

"I would love for you to join me if you could please."

Melita asked her husband. The two sat on the porch that evening and hoped for the best at the last arguments of Kharma's trial for the following day.

"Court is now in session, all rise the honorable Judge Mathers Presiding."

"You all may be seated, okay we are here today as you all may know this is the last Deliberation of the People vs.

Gomez trial each attorney will argue their last plea afterwards the jury will decided what's true and what is not, with that being said Attorney Mack you may state your plea first."

"Thank you your honor, I would like to take this time instead to allow Kharma Gomez, the accused, to reflect on this situation if it pleases the court your honor?"

"The court will allow it, Ms. Gomez you may now state your plea," the judge permitted Kharma.

Kharma stood up from her seat and faced the court.

"I am not going to beg for your sympathy, I am well aware that my actions had consequences. I will not stand here and play victim nor will I point blame. I fell for Adam; I knew very well that he was married but I was selfish, young, and naive. I was not alone in my feelings, this man of whom so many of you respected, had my mind. Most of all my heart, and I can honestly say he loved me too. I have his son. He is my all, my pride, and my joy. I am ashamed to say that in suffering from heartbreak and postpartum depression), I neglected him which is something that I will forever regret. Before you all play god with my life I would like for you all to hear something."

Kharma turned to her attorney as the judge nodded she pushed play on the recorder.

The Recording:

"Did you stick to the story? Listen keep it together do not blow this Kharma remember stick to our plan. Do not tell anyone that I killed that bastard let's keep the plot going of you killing him and taking the fall. You will get a slap on the hand if you plead insanity."

As the recording ended the entire court room got quiet. Kharma looked over at Timothy and Miss Carlene who gave her smiles and a nod. Kharma took her seat as she caught glimpse of Lana giving her looks that could kill.

"Your honor if it pleases the court I would also call Mr. Lewis he is the powered attorney for the deceased's estate"

"Allowed" the Judge replied

"Mr. Lewis would you please come to the front of the court room please and read the last words of Mayor Adam D Harris," Mack addressed Adam's attorney.

Mr. Lewis made his way to the front of the court room and began to read a letter from Adam.

"It is with my deepest apologies that I could not be here at the reading of this letter reasons for being are because I hurt

those that loved me and either I left this town for good or someone very dear to me took my life for breaking their heart. Kharma I loved you. Being with you was no mistake at all. I never, God knows I never meant to break your heart or lead you on by any means. When you told me you were pregnant I was really overjoyed and wanted nothing more than to be there when our child would be born. Things were not as they seemed as my hands were tied in this matter. My lovely wife threaten to take my children away, along with everything I have ever worked for if I didn't end this thing with you and deny and our unborn child. I regret this daily and I only hoped that I could've had the chance to meet him. In the event of my death Kharma you will be the owner of my estate; there will also be a piece in there for our son including AJ and Aimee."

Love Always,

Adam

After reading the letter Mr. Lewis returned to his seat. "I rest my case your honor," Mack stated and took his seat.

Harper looked over at Lana Harris and back at Kharma "Your honor it seems that this trial has taken an unseen turn, therefore to end this WILL MY SURPRISE WITNESS PLEASE

STEP FORWARD AT THIS TIME?" everyone turned to the double doors as they opened there was a huge gasp let out all over the court room

"Will you please state your name for the court?"

"Yes, Kacey Armani" the young woman stated glancing over at Kharma giving her a wink.

"Personally I have nothing to add to this case other than Lana Harris deserves everything she gets, which is not a lot considering that my girl just won all those coins. Who's the dumb bitch now Lana?!"

"Your honor I rest my case," Harper stated. Lana had no idea that the entire time Kharma was on to her plans to have her put away for the murder of Adam and no intentions of sharing anything with her or Ka'Son. So she and her bestie Kacey plotted against her, from Kacey sleeping with Adam to Kacey's staged death.

"Your honor I will testify that Lana Harris plotted this entire thing in exchange for no jail time I will be willing to undergo psychiatric help and parenting classes so long as I will be able to return to my son after my treatments are successful."

Kharma pleaded with the judge.

"Agreed, Deputy take Mrs. Harris away a later trial date will be set for her!" Lana stood in a trance as the cuffs were placed on her and she was taken away.

"Mommy!" her kids called out to her, as her parents Sidney and Albert held on to their grandchildren escorting them out the court room. Kharma ran to her family and hugged them all. She held on to her mother tightly and whispered into her ear "I am my mother's daughter, I love you mom".

Kharma walked over to Miss Carlene and before she could open her mouth to speak the kind and mother like elderly woman answered her question for her "Yes child of course I will be more than happy to take care of Ka'Son while you get yourself together; you go on do what you have to he is in great hands."

"Thank you" she gratefully replied to Miss Carlene. As she was being taken out by the courts appointed psychologist she turned to glance at Timothy who mouthed the words, *"Will You Marry Me?" to her and in her response to his question she nodded "Yes."* Timothy was overjoyed as he shook Sebastian's hand and hugged Melita while giving Alonzo a high five. Once outside the warmth of the sun hit

Kharma's face in that very moment she knew that this was her happy ending she had dreamed about.

The End

ORDER FORM
DIAMANTE' PUBLICATIONS, LLC
P.O. BOX 1034
Stone Mountain, GA 30086

Name (please print):_____

Address:_____

City/State: _____

Zip: _____

QTY	TITLES	PRICE

ORDER FORM

DIAMANTE' PUBLICATIONS, LLC
P.O. BOX 1034
Stone Mountain, GA 30086

Name (please print):_____

Address:_____

City/State: _____

Zip: _____

QTY	TITLES	PRICE
	KHARMA'S CHILD	$15
	FLATLINED 1	$20
	FLATLINED 2	$20
	GHETTO GOSPELS 1	$12
	GHETTO GOSPELS 2	$12
	BRIDAL BLISS	$20
	CRUMBLING DOWN	$15
	LADY GOONZ	$15

ORDER FORM

DIAMANTE' PUBLICATIONS, LLC
P.O. BOX 1034
Stone Mountain, GA 30086

Name (please print):_____

Address:_____

City/State: _____

Zip: _____

QTY	TITLES	PRICE
	LADY GOONZ 2	$15
	LACED PANTIES	$10
	UNBREAKABLE TIES	$15
	DOPE	$15
	TRIPLE CROSS	$15
	THE POWER OF V	$15

ORDER FORM
DIAMANTE' PUBLICATIONS, LLC
P.O. BOX 1034
Stone Mountain, GA 30086

Name (please print):_____

Address:_____

City/State: _____

Zip: _____

TEEN/CHILDREN:

QTY	TITLES	PRICE
	THROUGH OUR EYES	$10
	AJ'S WISH	$10
	ONE DAY: A BULLYING STORY	$10

Shipping and handling: add $3.00 for 1st book. Then $1.00 for each additional book.

Please allow 2-4 weeks for delivery.

Stay Tuned as Diamante' Publications has plenty more heat for you

Join our mailing list
diamantepublications@gmail.com

To see what's releasing next, read a sneak peek or win great prizes

YOU CAN ALSO VISIT US AT
www.diamantepublications.com

54816506R00132

Made in the USA
Charleston, SC
13 April 2016